# Venicia in the Cause of Aircraft

JONATHAN LOVEJOY

Armageddon Publishing

Cover: *Mimosa*, 1899
William Adolphe Bouguereau (1825-1905)

ISBN-10: 0692429298
ISBN-13: 978-0692429297

*For every Laura*

*And I will show wonders in heaven above, and signs in the earth beneath; blood, and fire, and vapour of smoke.*

Acts 2:19

# The Mommy Game

My DAUGHTER made her first plane crash when she was only five years old.

THE STARS on this clear, Kansas night remind me of the first time I saw it happen.

This arm of the Milky Way reaches down to my pathetic condition. Grabbing me helpless and unawares, to place me inside the heart of memory against my will, so that I am again burdened by the sight and sound of fire and nighttime vapour of smoke. And the irony is that I moved out here from the suburban silliness to get away from the end of the world that I sensed was coming, as it was foretold to me by human behavior.

Desperate Housewife Syndrome and workaholic husbands. Women doing the bunny hop from bed to bed like it was game. Men so obsessed with FICO scores and money that they work 16 hours a day and another 8 on Saturday. Children being scheduled into premature exhaustion before they even get to high school. Seventeen year old daughters being stripped and whipped behind closed doors with their mother's belts, as per the beautiful, busty cheerleader who showed up at my door in the evening day, slamming on it like she was running from a German Shepherd, begging me to please open the door and let her in. A teenage beauty with the biggest, prettiest eyes (and breasts) in the neighborhood, telling me that she had to run because her mother was going to beat her with the belt again, having made her strip naked as usual, the girl having lost her nerve this time and ran from the cause of leather on her skin. The girl's gigantic breasts keep flopping around in my memory, which keeps saying to my groin over and over again, how lucky her husband is going to be, or her boyfriend already, whoever he is.

Sometimes I think about that big breasted, yellow skinned beauty. What secrets her black father was oblivious to, concerning the girl and her white mother. As it is written, it would cause an apocalyptic shock, the things that churn beneath cultured civility. It was as if I were somehow being shown this strange end of the world truth, that this perfect bodied, perfect beauty, with the blonde, blue eyed supermodel looking mother was being breast raped on a regular basis behind closed doors—this, by a flat chested beauty queen of a mother, who had been sucking on her daughter's tits since the girl was 13 years old, a stretch of four years to where the girl was now standing in my living room in a pair of my old jeans and T shirt. The girl's name was Dominique, I remember, half a generation ago. The things that girl told me still ache my groin to this day and night, her mother's extreme breast obsession not being the least among them. She told me that her mother's favorite thing to do was

5

to make the girl go topless, so that she could nurse on both of them, while Dominique pinched both her mother's *"giant nipples,"* the girl called them, which would cause the woman to have a thundering orgasm. Every time. At least once a month since the girl was thirteen, she said, this happened.

Oddly enough, I can remember when this girl was thirteen. Looking seventeen already back then in face and body, having taken after her statuesque, giraffe legged mother in raw beauty of expression. The sight of this cultured, suburban show wife would always fill me with quiet awe after that, and though I don't really know exactly why, seemed to be the last straw the camel's back could endure. The phony, happy go lucky smiles she had, pony tail bouncing in her jogging and walking up and down our neighborhood streets to see and be seen, not caring at all that somebody in the neighborhood might know her apocalyptic secret, that she is a mother lover, who turned her daughter into a motheress way back when she was thirteen.

*"I don't know what Dominique may have told you,"* she says, *"but let me apologize for her because she lies like a dog on a living room carpet,"* she told me. *"She breaks curfew, she slacks off in school, she tries to see boys behind our back, she won't do chores when I ask, and then she can't take it when she has to be punished. I'm sorry if she gave you the wrong impression."*

*"No, its fine,"* I had said, my own smile beaming fungalooga white, *"she just told me she was scared, that's all. I got whippings myself when I was growing up, so I understand."* Which is as completely true as anything, I'm afraid, as my back still itches sometimes from the memory of my own mother's anger.

Within the year, my four year old and I were gone. Out here on the Kansas Prairie, where the world is at times a rolling sea of green, where the reality of the coming apocalypse does not burn so bright. But the stars of the Milky Way Galaxy beckon, to burden me again with the truth that there is no escape from the truth. That the rumble of thunder is louder away from the clamour of human noise, and the messages in the stars are more clearly read, away from the ambient lights of the city.

I am reminded of my time at the kitchen window one particular night, when I saw a fireball streaking slowly across the sky, enough that I had to run outside, where my five year old daughter was standing in the middle of our back yard, overlooking the ocean plain of wheat, watching this great fireball streak from the top of the sky all the way down to the bottom, where it died in an explosion of booming light and sound.

## 3

ARE THERE OTHER MOTHERS such as I, who are scared to death of their own daughters? And strangely enough, it wasn't the fiery crashes that first lit the flames of fear inside me. She didn't crash another one until she was twelve. This fear was ignited inside me when she was only nine years old, when she had slept in the same bed with me overnight. She had clung unnaturally close to me all night, which seemed so very natural to her that I wondered who she had done this with before, but knowing already inside myself there was no one. Even in the morning before she woke up, I woke up on my back with her clamped to my body fast asleep, her leg draped over me and her arm tightly around my middle, her head laid down upon the cushion of my breast without apology, the side of her little nine year old face pressed tightly against one of my gargantuans, one of the "big pillows" as she calls them. Even

*"Have you been kissing somebody like this?"* I say, wondering what babysitter or older sister at some sleepover has been teaching my daughter behind my back.

*"I'm kissing* you *like this,"* she says. And as if to punish my audacity, this little nine year old grown up gets to her knees above me, and actually takes her nightshirt completely off, and then slides her underwear off and throws them to the floor on the same side of the bed as where the big shirt lays out of sight.

I can only stare in total awe and end of the world bewilderment, as she sits on top of me astraddle with no clothes on, unbuttoning my pajama top to expose the big pillows, one of which she takes by both hands, leans down and proceeds to pull the nipple up into her mouth like a human vacuum cleaner, which shoots a lightning spark directly to my groin, that threatens to make me have to piss a flood onto these sheets.

*"Who taught you to do this,"* I say, as if I really cared. *"I asked you a question young l— "*

And the self righteous, hypocritical "lady" word is cut off when she moves from my breast to my mouth again, laying down on top of me in a strength and heaviness well beyond her years, pushing my breasts together up under her body, then proceeding to grind herself against my pajama bottoms while looking directly at me.

I am in too much shock and awe to speak. Wondering how it is that both my tits are so apocalyptically sensitive all of a sudden, and why I have such a strong urge to flood these sheets underneath her. Her little awkward grinding and moving her body around on my breasts is The Mommy Game to her to be sure, but to my body it is of the utmost seriousness, and I wonder how many more of her stiff little movements it is going to take before I start shaking and wetting these sheets like a glass of water in an earthquake.

But fortunately (or unfortunately), the girl is inspired to stop moving and to slide my pajama bottoms off. Then she coaxes me out of my open pajama top, which I ashamedly submit to, embarrassed as she takes a charge of me that I had never imagined possible, whispering to me to open my legs, which I do in total guilt, spreading my legs open and holding them back, as my daughter begins to press and grind herself with less naiveté than before, responding to her own body's arousal this time, which has twisted her pretty little features into something akin to pain and confusion.

And in the mist of her little girl bewilderment, upon this forbidden awakening in her body, she pins my arms to my sides so that they are *immobile*, and she sucks one great nipple into her mouth and holds it there, while she begins to endure her body's inherent understanding, a feeling passed to her from somewhere along the timeline, from this selfsame tragedy passed from my mother to me when I was much older, her body now possessed by an automatic rhythm, unique to this moment in the history of the world, where she begins to breathe so hard through her nose that I know she needs more air, suddenly opening her mouth so she can breathe through the trauma as she humps herself into me in fascinating 5/4 time, breathing open mouthed upon my breasts as she pounds into me with otherworldly strength from her small body, until her rhythm is sparked to a sudden change, causing her to jerk and spasm, amidst the sound of three loud and girlish shrieks that leap from her body into the air around us. But even so, she cannot stop moving, and clamps her lips back to my breast as she finishes her shaking, the feel of which sends a line from my nipple to somewhere beyond my groin, and I am aware of only the fact that there is a God, and he is having no mercy on my body at this moment in time.

$\mathcal{I}$ AM afraid of my daughter.

To speak a more apocalyptic understatement is rare indeed. Forget about the fact that she has turned this part of the world into the new Bermuda Triangle of airplane crashes. This goes all the way back to when she was just twelve years old, and laid on top of me, and I realized that I couldn't move. And she was not the least bit angry or upset. I don't mean that I couldn't get up. I could not *move*. It was a condition beyond paralysis, as though I were inside a waking dream, where a person is made to understand that the types of fear are many, and uniquely distinguished. Among these is the Fear of Demons, a.k.a. Fear of the Supernatural, where the dreamer is in grieving to move a muscle, to twitch and jerk just enough, so that the safety of awakening can be achieved. Maybe I was being punished for what I had allowed to happen, I don't know. But it happened in the tranquility of Sunday Morning, after The Mommy Game had been played again, where I had suffered the trauma of another orgasm from Pandora's Box, which had me wailing a siren into the Saturday night walls.

In keeping with what mischievous betrayal a twelve year old girl is capable of, she had rolled over on top of me that morning with the strangest look on her face, as if she were nearly tickled by a secret she knew. And oh, what secrets from the end of the age have been bestowed, upon a child who has laid in depravity with her mother! Venicia's body is suddenly weighted down so heavy on top of me I can barely breathe, which brings the giggly, good natured *"let Mommy up, baby, I can't breathe."* But when I say this, she only repositions herself on top of me, until I feel like I am a prisoner of some malevolent, unseen force that couldn't be escaped from in a hundred years.

What of invisible shackles and big, strong, angry men, of what fearfulness or harm can they cause? I know that what holds me down is the weight of centuries, a touch of evil from beyond what we can see, and I know that somehow, I'm wide awake, I cannot move a muscle, and it is being caused by my mischievous 12 year old daughter.

*"Venicia, let Momma up, I can't move."* But Venicia lays on top of me unresponsive, as if she threatens to go back to sleep, and use me as a body pillow for God knows how long.

And suddenly, I am acquainted with that well known fear, the kind so intense that it causes physical pain in the body, sparking every nerve in my body to panic, where I can feel my heart fluttering and skipping a beat or two, as it begins to pump ice cold blood through my veins.

*"Venicia please, I can't move. Venicia please! VENICIA!"*

And even though my daughter is now aware of the sound of a death scream, she lays there for many seconds more, feeling, hearing the nature of terror expressed from the human heart, the unique power of it released into 3D space, until at last I claw myself into motion, done by her reluctant mercy, and I push her off of me and sit up in the bed, holding my chest and pulling in the deepest breaths I possibly can. Realizing that no, I am not waking up from a dream, nor some prescription induced bout of morning insanity. I turn to look at my little 12 year old Carmen doll, my little brunette exotic, Mediterranean looks from her bygone father, laying there as calm as the seashore on a sunny day, staring at me without a smile, nor a single word of comfort or explanation.

# From the Heart of a Seven Year Slumber

 MY DAUGHTER was twelve, when the sprit came to her. My daughter is twelve, when the spirit hath come.

The odds of dying in a plane crash are at least  eight million to one, they say. The odds of lightning striking the earth twice in the same place carries the same weight of impossibility, I suppose. Unless you are a skyscraper in a lightning storm, holding your hopelessness pointed in spire to the sky.

What are the odds of a plane crashing in a wheat field in Topeka, Kansas? What are the odds of it happening again, seven years later, upon the accursed ground of the same space in time? In the heart of memory, I can see the little brunette beauty from the patio door of the kitchen. Engaged in her favorite hobby, which is training her gaze into the sky, far down to every horizon, watching the airplanes glide smoothly across the open sea of blue, leaving the trail of white smoke behind them in the sky. I wondered sometimes if she was ever as naïve as me, believing that the clouds themselves are born from this, as I believed at least once when I was a girl.

I try to keep myself from disturbing the foundation she is building, the protection she must surely be giving her psychology, against the fiery recollection from her early childhood, when the plane exploded no more than five miles west of our back door. Although she has never mentioned it, I know that her mind somehow allows her to cope with the memory that haunts her like a dream, of the fireball that fell like a comet from the sky. Does she remember it as anything more than just a dream? I am forced to wonder myself at times, did it really happen? And if I am ever struck with this doubt hard enough, I refer to the newspaper clippings from the *Topeka Chronicle,* which tells me that no, I am not some ghostly figure adrift in the gray world, but I am a living, breathing extension of reality. And yes, the cold that churns the pit of my stomach is real, and the memories of the fiery crash, The Mommy Game, and the way she held me still on my back really did happen.

This three pronged attack will not let me be on this warm summer morning, as I stand at the back patio door. Having to admit to myself that this impossibly pretty and somber little girl is about a strange as they come. Maybe, she has within her the seeds of travel, imagining that she might someday ride the wind from here to nowhere. Maybe, she is delighted by the science of what she sees, of the air and the sky itself, alongside the impossibility of manmade flight, and what laws and equations bring it into being. Or maybe, her little spirit processes the world through melancholy, building within her a reservoir of words, where someday the world might read of the Atwood verses, where *his colors are the sky and the sea, the grass, and the leaves of every tree.* Which of these, if any, burns the Venician mind with wonder, as she surveys the summer skies above us without ceasing? All I know at this moment is what haunts my mind like a ghost in the halls of an abandoned house, that even though she is a weak little girl half my size, she held me down with the unbridled strength of 10 men and beyond, into the territory of full blown paralysis upon me down to the muscle and bone.

I am suddenly annoyed at myself, for being afraid to speak to my own twelve year old daughter. I push through this tangible veil of fear, shooing these spirits of morning dread aside, sliding the back door open with authority, walking out into the Kansas morning air. The breeze blows leisurely off the open prairie, from beyond the small groves of trees in the far distance, waving the stalks of golden wheat in ripples of contemplation and warning. The breeze flows from the surface atop the sea of grain, across the grass of our isolated lawn and property.

Maybe, it is the size of our little two bedroom brick house, I don't know, that allowed it to be vacant in the first place, when we came looking for our paradise seven years ago.

*"How many planes have you counted?"* I ask, looking dimly into the open blue sky, barely noticing the trails of white meditation present, even mistaking them as wisps of high altitude clouds drifting by. Without a

word, Venicia points to the widened wisp of feathery white, stretched across the length of sky down to the western blue.

*"Is that the only one,"* I say. Trying to imagine briefly who in the world they were, and where in the world in their silver flight they are going.

*"Venicia...do you remember when you were on top of Mommy? In my bed?"*

*"You mean The Mommy Game?"*

*"No. I mean, when you were laid on top of me...with our clothes* on."

I say it with enough stealth to qualify it as a loud whisper. As if the very stalks of summer wheat are in grieving to listen.

*"Do you remember?"*

I see her tuck her little full, pink lips in, pretending to be concentrating again on the sky.

*"How did you hold Mommy down like that, so that I couldn't move?"*

In her silence, I see, is contained the echo of the same apprehension I feel.

*"Can you tell Mommy how you did it?"*

*"Did what?"*

*"Held me down like that so that I couldn't move. It scared me so bad, I screamed. Remember?"*

*"Can we have sausage and waffles?"*

Briefly, I am shocked away from foolishness. To attend to the reality of breakfast, and moving on from silly fears and fantasies.

Briefly.

*"Venicia, I want you to answer me. How did you do that?"*

*"I was just playing, Mommy."*

*"But... how were you playing? How did you..."*

And suddenly, I realize that I couldn't possibly expect the child to know what I'm talking about, let alone give me any kind of an answer I can use.

*"I'm sorry, sweetie."*

I pull her close to me, pressing her face to my comfort cushions in D minor, glad that there are no barriers left between us that we cannot climb.

*"I'll go cook your breakfast, You want to stay out here and look for airplanes?"*

She nods her head, lips tucked in again, briefly pointing towards the far and distant northern horizon, to the far left of our backyard western view.

Barely glimpsing the new trail of white in the blue sky, I touch her face with both hands, bending down to kiss her full on the mouth—a kiss without pretense or hesitation, that no manner what mysteries we encounter in our little world, between us will be no secrets, nor walls of emotional resistance to bear.

In the kitchen, I set about the task of *Eggo* and *Jimmy Dean,* to give my little Venicia cause to enjoy the rest of her summer morning, and my self cause to be five to seven pounds heavier about the hips. The orange juice will be sweet and then sour as we eat—sweet after the taste of sausage, then sour when the buttery sweetness of the waffles has come and gone.

A glimpse out the window overwhelms me with déjà vu, as I can now see the air plane looking many times bigger than it had a few minutes ago. I am suddenly entranced by the oddest of sights, which is a huge passenger jet turned on its side, descending toward the ground at an angle somewhere way beyond diagonal, until the words *vertical* and *perpendicular* threaten. It is a sight that begs a flight to the nearest door, so that every inch of this benchmark in time can be recorded in tragic memory.

I hurry from the kitchen stove to the patio door, stepping into the daytime version of a nighttime terror I saw seven years ago, this time with my daughter being twelve years old instead of five, watching what looks like the largest passenger jet in the world in tragic and rapid descent toward the ground, looking as though it is flying intentionally toward the Kansas wheat field, close enough that the thunderous engines are loud and clear, as the plane dives into the golden sea of grain, disappearing into the Golden Sea, marked by a rumble as deep as an earthquake, and a ball of fire exploding into the air like something from the mouth of a fire breathing dragon, disturbed from the heart of a seven year slumber.

$\mathcal{T}$HE PLUMES OF REVELATION arise in billowing fire and vapour of smoke, leaving the remains of a mushroom cloud at our Western Horizon. I am burdened by the overwhelming spirit of apocalypse, and the looming spectre of impending doom. I decide not to go anywhere near this tragedy, neither in body nor spirit, taking Venicia by the arm and escorting her somewhat angrily into the house. Even she says fearfully, *"should we call 911,"* to which I respond, *"they'll be here soon enough, honey."*

*"Did they all get killed?"* she asks, her face in deep anguish and turmoil.

*"I think they all did sweetie...nobody could have survived that explosion."*

Venicia suddenly grabs onto me around the waist, weeping bitterly against my chest. *"I didn't want them to get killed,"* she says, a voice so pitiful that it judges me, convicting me of Bad Mother Syndrome, for allowing her to stand there and watch it happen in the first place. But how was I to stop her from looking, when I couldn't even move to stop myself?

*"Everything will be alright, sweetie. Just say a prayer in your heart for them. Ask God to take them to Heaven."*

But the works are of little comfort to her crying, dying spirit, prompting me to hold her face up to me, so that I can stare her directly in the eyes. And in keeping with what spirits have flown from Pandora's Box unlocked and opened in our lives, I lean down and kiss her firmly on the mouth, lingering, until the kiss moves beyond the innocence of comfort, to spark instincts from my Triangle of Needs, from my breasts, to my bowels, to somewhere in my womb and beyond.

I take my little Carmen Doll by the hand, escorting her unashamedly, unabashedly away from our abandoned kitchen feast, then up the stairs, to the hidden safety of our upper room. *It is a once in a lifetime opportunity,* my corrupted soul says to me, and I know that I must strike while the iron is hot, to nurture the growing, the glowing of this eternal flame, which is the burning of blue and black fire.

I sit down on the edge of my bed, pulling her squishy young body in close to me, staring deeply into her beautiful eyes, nearly Egyptian in their exotic intent, but being fully Italian, passed down from her bygone father's Mother, a full blooded Italian beauty, who endured the accusation *witch* more than once throughout her life. The deep,

I stare down at her, noticing her match my stare, while she begins to take hold of my other breast, squeezing it gently with her hand. *"Close your eyes, baby,"* I say, brushing them closed gently, feeling each pull of her suckling lips and tongue lift me higher and higher up and away, drifting me across the prairie to the scattered remains of smoldering technology, and the bodies of 309 people spread out all over creation.

# The Beauty of White Tigers

SIX WEEKS have moved us along the timeline, deeper into the heart of summer. We are nursemaids, my daughter and me, as she has drank her fill at least a dozen times since the milk started to flow. From D minor to D Major, up into the key of F these bosoms of mine have risen forth, to provide my daughter and me with an end of the world secret, an apocalyptic expression of want and need, where her 12 year old desire is often obsessive. Naked or clothed, sitting or standing, in the kitchen or the bathroom, these milk jugs are hers to play with, to have as a source of nourishment for her mind and body. We share something so private, perhaps so rare that it can never be discussed with another human being than ourselves, nor would anyone be inclined to believe it anyway. One of our favorite thins to do is to whisper into each other's ear loudly in public the words *"milk, milk, milk,"* over and over again, to make the moms and daughters around us wonder what manner of secret we share, both of us loving the tingle of this breathy little secret, as it tickles our ears with knowledge of the forbidden.

Five o'clock traffic snarls our sojourn out of the city, after a day of walking and shopping in Topeka, us holding hands from one end of the giant mall to the other, until there were just too many bags for us to buy another thing, so many of them dolls to add to Venicia's Barbie collection, already grown past twenty after today. How long before the smiling, empty headed things are in the attic and forgotten, truly I do not know. The danger is that she does not take them out of the boxes without returning them in perfect order, in true collector fashion, though she is only twelve years old, never leaving them wild haired, naked and scattered about her bedroom floor in an orgy of blonde hair and plastic breasts exposed.

The beauty of white tigers and golden evening gowns whirls a gig in my brain, as the jumbo jet drifts slowly toward the traffic-snarled, five o'clock highway. The sheer, otherworldly size of the dreadful thing makes me have to touch my daughters leg, as she gazes fearfully out her passenger window as if it is going to crash right in front of us. What lifetime traumas have been burned into her poor brain, down into her accursed soul, having been struck by the lightning of apocalyptic tragedy? What did our white tigers at the zoo know of us, as they lost interest in their own little world? As the two of them wandered over to the edge of the glass where we were, and stared into Venicia's face as if in grieving to ask her a question?

The eyes of the tiger burn white in my memory, as the jumbo jet airplane drifts the passengers in latter day leisure toward the airport, somewhere on the other side of the city. When suddenly, my casual view in the windshield cracks loudly from top to bottom, followed by a blast of fiery orange white in a thunderous noise, causing me to scream from the cold prick of my heart and lungs, holding both hands over my mouth as the noise cascades around us like thunder, shaking the car and rattling us to the bone, as the burning fireball passes over the congested highway in a trail of billowing flame and smoke, crashing into the small, grassy field and forest grove so close by, missing the road by what seems to be mere inches, rolling along the ground as a living blob of liquid fire with an internal life of its own.

The world as we know it ends in a *blast* of thunderous sound, as I hold on to my daughter, listening to the breaking of her psychology flow out from her in a repeated *"I'm sorry, I'm sorry, I'm sorry..."*

I look at her with as much rapt bewilderment as at this third bolt of lightning into our nightmare world, yelling at her in the loss of my own control *"Its alright honey, its alright!"* Pulling her tight to the milk filled bosom of mine, pressing her face to them as she cries uncontrollably, turning in time to see the fire on the ground blast the smoke and orange flame into a ball of white, liquid heat energy again, sending another burst of thunder through every heart on this five o clock highway, and the fear of eschatology through every lost and wayward soul.

*M*Y *DAUGHTER is insane...*

In the rising darkness of our upper room, as the earth turns toward the evening day, I sit at the edge of my bed, where my daughter is comfortable enough to rest. I can only wonder what part I have played in this seven year dismantling of her little psychology, and why Fate seems to have chosen to drive her out of her mind. I sit at the edge of reason, an hour removed from the nursing I coaxed her into, which I knew would relax her back into our reality, where she does not have to cringe in fear at the mere thought of a passing airplane, and she does not have to believe that somehow, she is the cause of what we saw today.

I stroke my 12 year old beauty's hair in the guise of motherhood, where my comforting of her is not ensconsed in selfish instinct, and the need for the unmentionable coursing like a river through my body. But even as I begin to worry for her sanity, I know that this night especially, I am going to crush this little girl flat of her back with my naked body, until I am shaking like ground zero at the start of World War Three. To be raised up on my arms high above her, with my udders hung down in her face, with my big groin pressed to her little hairless groin is the sweet tart apple pie of my body's craving, and as surely as I am alive and breathing, I am going to make it happen.

But for now, what comfort I can provide is about as unselfish as I can make it, I think. Stroking her hair as she drifts into a state just beyond rest, into the edges of a deeper, and more steady breathing. This, I see happening to her, suddenly interrupted by her opening her eyes and saying aloud *"I didn't mean to cause it."* I reach down to her smooth, ivory little cheek with a gentle kiss, whispering shushes and reassurances that she is not an end of the world jinx, and no, she did not cause the plane to blow up right in front of us, nor did she cause the one from six weeks ago to crash in our field out back, and no, she did not cause the nighttime earth comet to blaze to the ground when she was five.

But can I ever allow her into the arms of so-called "professional help," knowing what I do (about what we do)? It is a secret that we will carry to our graves, to be sure, and whatever psychological help we need to escape insanity, surely we can provide. Surely, we can.

*"I have to tell you something, Mommy? Because I don't want it to happen again."*

*"Don't want what to happen again, sweetie?"*

*"The airplanes."*

*"Venicia, you don't have to say that anymore. Those crashes are not your fault. How can they be? You're starting to worry me a little bit, honey. Because if I didn't know any better, I'd say that you really believed it."*

*"But I do believe it, Mommy. I do."*

*"Venicia..."*

*"Mommy, I can—"*

For whatever reason, some revelations have a barrier that must be crossed. Either in the telling, or the reception.

What is the third part of the truth?

Is it cataclysm?

*"The first dream I remember having,"* she says, *"was before we moved here. I dreamed that I was in a place that looked just like where we live, like a big, open field. I saw a big plane flying by, and I reached up at it, and it stopped moving. And I was able to make it move back and forth in the dream. It was like it was a toy, and I could control it. And when I woke up, I felt like I was already awake, and had never been to sleep. It didn't feel like a dream."*

When I shake my head in denial, she can hardly know it is to block the words *"a vision"* from taking hold in my mind.

*"Honey, it was just a dream. It wasn't real."*

*"But it felt real. I felt like I was connected to the plane. Like I could make it do whatever I wanted it to do."*

*"Honey, just because you had a dream..."*

*"Remember when you couldn't move that day?"*

*"What about it?"*

*"You asked me how I did it?"*

35

*"How* did *you do it?"*

*"I did it with my mind, Mommy."*

Bad luck is the child of premature ambition. This applies to every feeble attempt at success before the time is right. Everything from taking an egg off the fire before its ready, to a failed run for the White House. If its not meant for it to happen yet, there are buzzards and black cats all over the place.

As to her attempt to make me process this, there are no doves and deer nearby.

*"With your mind?"*

*"Yes, Mommy."*

*"How?"*

*"That's the only way I know how to say it. With my mind. And its strong, Mommy. Its stronger than you can imagine."*

# The Dancing Dolls of Atwood

# *9*

" *I*TS GOT NOTHING TO DO WITH SATAN
*Momma, it's me... If I concentrate hard
enough I can move things..."*

I listen to the end of the world sermon preached from the movie I found in the early evening browsing, while Venicia languishes somewhere up the stairs, likely ruling court over her Barbie Doll legion. For some reason, as I watch the movie girl misfit prophecy to a latter day generation of what fearful things are coming upon the earth in fire and blood, I am struck with a spark of fear, as I suddenly imagine the Dancing Dolls of Atwood, and what clumsy or elegant gliding or twirling they might be performing out of my sight.

Part of me wants to confront this nonsense directly. To go upstairs and threaten to bare her bottom to my bare hand if she persists, then comfort her later with my sickness and perversion. But it is the other part of me that makes me turn the volume down on my end of the world movie, even though the prom prophecy in fire and blood are pending, and the revelation of what happens when a real witch gets angry. I get up from my cushion comfort repose, to go out back into the cool, Kansas summer night.

If the facts of what actually happened are faced, what do we have? One, a plane crashed in our field when my daughter was five, and she was watching it when it happened. Two, another place crashed in this same field six weeks ago, and my daughter was watching it when it happened. Three, a jumbo jet exploded and crashed right in front of us on the highway this afternoon... and my daughter watched it happen. Four, she held me down with the strength of 10 men that morning.

So, what conclusions can I draw? Truthfully, none. And even if she *can* move things with her mind, how can she do something as impossible as make an airplane crash?

High above the nighttime prairie field, among the twinkling stars aplenty, I see no less than three sets of tiny blinking lights, gliding peacefully across the darkened sky. I am suddenly struck with an idea, to try and put this foolishness to rest. I go back inside to the foot of the stairs, calling out her name, refusing to go upstairs to her room, because truthfully, I have no nerves for the sight of ten dolls standing up in the middle of the floor with no doll stands, all falling at once when I open the door.

I call her name again, this time with more determination, waiting until I hear the door to her room open. She appears at the top of the stairs quietly, strangely aware in her expression, as if she knows that we have finally arrived. That this part of the timeline is where the rubber hits the road, and we will gather momentum toward the truth without compromise.

Reluctantly, my brunette doll creeps down the stairs toward me in half obedience, almost as if I am the substance of dark premonition, the embodiment of her worst fears at the moment.

*"You okay?"* is the obligatory chirp from my corrupted mouth, as I take her hand, and walk with her from the living room through the kitchen, and out the sliding glass door into the Kansas prairie night.

*"I don't want any more of this airplane foolishness, Venicia. So, we're going to end it right here."*

My heart twinges with secret, sadistic delight, at the fear and dejection on her face.

I am in charge, little girl.

I am your mother.

*"After this, I never want to hear you speak about causing those airplane crashes again. Do you understand?"*

No answer.

*"I said, do you understand?"*

This, I draw from a different part of myself. Born from a youth spent in the shadow of the woman who gave me life, then took it from me so abundantly. *I said, do you understand* is the echo from somewhere along the timeline, in the heart of a distant suburban memory.

Far off in the north west corner of our sky, far to the right of our nighttime prairie view, it seems that one of the twinkling stars has begun to move, across the starlit western horizon.

*"You see that light moving? It's an airplane, or helicopter or something."*

*"I don't want to, Mommy."*

*"Of course you don't want to, because you can't. Can you? Can you?"*

Her lips tremble helplessly in the non answer. Her glimpse up at me would normally be heartbreaking.

But not tonight.

*"Look at me. If you ever mention this again, I will bare your bottom, and put you across my knee."*

*"I'll do it."*

*"What?"*

Without another word, she steps from the concrete patio, walking slowly toward the nighttime wheat field, stopping in the middle of the yard. Her audacity is amusing to say the least, causing me to settle down in one of the cushioned patio chairs, so I can watch her little farce crumble and fall, like a wall of ice off a glacier in the Bering Sea. I am amazed to the point of my jaw going slack, in open mouthed amazement as I watch her stand still in full concentration, with the most serious look on her beautiful little face, barely visible in the glow of our little space of ambient light.

At the height of my amusement, at my sadistic delight in watching her desperation to escape a spanking, she points with an authority beyond her years, and I glance in the direction of the moving light, seeing it flare into afireball among the stars.

I stand up in greater open mouthed amazement, understanding now that the world is at the end of the age, understanding that this is the twilight of humanity, as I watch the fireball streak in elegant tranquility toward the nighttime western horizon.

*T*HESE SMARMY, INSIPID, ENTITLED SUBURBAN WITCHES. You think you know what fear is? Your son cursed at you? Your powerless, pathetic little husband yelled at you?

I would like to introduce you to my daughter.

Without batting an eye…

She can break your fucking spine.

# 11

*I* STEPPED ON A CRACK—

*I broke my mother's back*

# The Death of a Maiden's Sanity

HE YEARS have passed into tragic oblivion, until my daughter has seen her sixteenth birthday, and Topeka has terrified the world as the Airline Graveyard. In the four years since I learned the truth about my daughter, thirty four airplanes have seen the souls of more than three thousand souls leave this world, on their way to the shores of Hell or Heaven.

All ambitions I have had towards a normal psychology have dried up, and blown away as dust in a prairie wind, as I now live my days and nights in fear. Is it because hardly a night goes by that I do not wake up in a panic sometime during the night, on the heels of some wicked premonition or another, where I will see dozens of souls screaming in the midst of fiery torment? Or perhaps a dream where I will feel the bones of my lower back stressed, as though they may snap in two.

The broken back dream must surely be my own psychology tormenting me, from the news of what happened back when she was only fifteen. On her very first day in the ninth grade, after having already grown into her sullen, somber self, a beautiful and prideful teacher, who had singled Venicia's name out for ridicule inexplicably during a roll call, calling her *Vernita Ackwood*, inciting more than one snicker from the junior varsity cheerleaders in class. When my daughter looked back at the blonde, private school faculty wannabe, cursed to teach 9<sup>th</sup> grade English to build a resume to add to her Master's Degree in Liberal Arts— when my daughter saw the teacher's smile slip from awkward merriment into abject mocking, she waited until the teacher was nearby the old classroom door with its big, ancient frosted glass window. At the moment of truth, the pencil in Venicia's hand snapped, and the teacher's body lurched forward in a loud *snap* that the whole class heard, and her head slammed through the glass in the door as if she had been thown. There, her body hung in well dressed, charcoal gray casual, slumped over the old wooden door where the glass used to be, every student stunned somewhere between shock and disbelief, wondering if they had witnessed some end of the world prank gone awry, or the remnants of a massive stroke that had sent her body flying.

And when I learned of this, when I learned that Venicia Marianna Atwood was there, I only had to look at her without breaking the stare, and I asked her without compromise, *"I just want to know why, and don't you lie to me."*

*"Because she laughed at me,"* Venicia had said. And she said it with a calmness—a controlled, mature determination far beyond herself, far

beyond her few years on this accursed earth. They said that the teacher's back was snapped like a broken tree limb, as if she had fallen from a great height onto a rounded metal railing. How did a fall through a glass onto a wooden door do that to her back? *"We heard it,"* some cheerleader girls had said, *"we heard something snap when she fell."*

And even a year beyond this incident, when my daughter has not agreed to be taken out of school, and isolated from the world, I still get soreness in my lower back when I think of the blonde, private school wannabe teacher, whose corpse now rests with a snapped spinal column inside her coffin.

In truth, I think Venicia's *physical* beauty is the last safety net between her and a total retreat from society, donning the mannerisms of the quiet, smart brunette beauty, escaping complete ostracization because of her looks alone, though the blue ribbon club still looks upon her with suspicion and mild disdain, simply because she is so quiet and is very much a loner. She is, by far, even at 16 years old, the most beautiful girl or woman in the entire high school, looking all of 23 years old when she wears makeup, with a body that is truly devastation to look upon. With a pleasant smile from behind her goth moodiness, unafraid to show her curves in tight t-shirts and jeans, Venicia Atwood is a natural curiosity at best, a wonder for them to behold, who is unashamed to walk with the geeks and nerd girls down the halls between classes, and who has a genuine smile for even the boys with no hope who speak to her. It might be safe to say that aside from the jealous clique, the girls who wish to be the prettiest but can't be because of Venicia Atwood—aside from this jealous few, she is pretty much left alone, which is indeed an answer to a poor mother's prayer.

If Bethany Gary should ride the wind, would she be a fireball in the sky? Bethany is the school queen bee, who carries a poisoned sting. And from what I know, I  know that if my daughter stays on that campus, Bethany will probably not live to receive her diploma on graduation day.

# 13

$\mathcal{N}$O LESS THAN FIVE of her sixteen and seventeen year old friends decorate the living room like living dolls, if they can truly be called friends, for I know that their interest in my daughter is purely cosmetic, and for what prestige can be gathered from within. Here at the end of my daughter's 10th grade year, at the edge of another summer season, Bethany Gary, Brittany Hale, Bridgette McLaughlin, Caitlyn Stevens and Amber Hall have been able to resist no more, with sixteen year old Bethany Gary being the center of it all, leading the charge of this light brigade, to be the first group to get a hold of the quiet and impossibly beautiful Venicia Atwood, before the nerd clubs and super square geek girls lay claim to her.

Venicia's physical appearance is such that she has been the subject of whispers and speculation, who's her boyfriend, whose her girlfriend, which male teacher has she seduced, is she really dating half the football team, is she really a witch who can make her pencil jump up from her desk into her hand, was she really seen kissing a grown woman at the mall, whatever. But as is typical with the flow of inevitability, the powers that be have decided to recruit her into where she is meant to be—to pull her out of her shell of lonerism, to hopefully see her in a varsity cheerleader uniform at the beginning of next year, before the yearbook nerds and school government preps get their hands on her, burying her in a mountain of socially useless playacting and pretending to be grownups looking to rule the world before the age of 21. No. You are a living doll, dear Venicia. You are one of us. You will be the red flower on our white and yellow cake, you will be the diamond in our golden ring. Without effort, you will be a sequoia among pines, the queen among these young women and men. To say your name, to conjure images of you will be to summon power—the pride, privilege and prestige we will share. President of this and queen of that, leader of this and the head of that, until we are established in your court of rule, the queen whose face is Miss Universe, and whose body is Miss Hawaiian Tropic curved to a greater infinity.

Thou art the evidence that mankind once mated with angels, Venicia Marianna, as does one who was named Cyndi Crawford, in the days when the promise of the sky was still blue. Thou art this Italian Egyptian looking thing, which has terrified us all to grieving, and burned both our minds and bodies to devastation and ruin. The handsome athletes are of thee, Queen Venicia, surely, you cannot be wooed by them! The teachers old enough to be your father carry you into their dreams, as they lay beside their bitter, plain and frigid wives in sorrow! But your time has come, Queen Venicia, to take your place at our side, to raise our status higher than any class in the history of our school, when your pictures are recorded with us, and your name is burned into stone with ours, from here until the end of time.

From the kitchen, I hear a squeal of laughter coming from one of the Fab Five, poised on the edge of ruling the school, hoping to become the Sweet Six, before the advent of their eleventh grade year. I listen to the laughing and the giggling and the chattering, noticing a curious thing, that in twenty minutes of constant laughing and lying to themselves and one another, I don't hear Venicia's voice a single time.

Suddenly, the space of my little country kitchen is filled with W.A.S.P. hair and perfume, White And So Pretty girls looking and strolling like Heaven on Earth, all legs and smiles and at least one tremendous bosom or two, surrounding me in a barrage of blue eyed, white teethed phoniness that I can feel, gnawing at me like hungry she-wolves on a leg bone.

"Miss Atwood, Venicia was afraid to ask you, but we're having a sleep over tonight at my house, you can even call my Mom and ask her. Venicia wants to come with us but she was too scared to ask you. Would it be okay if she went with us? We were getting ready to leave before it gets too dark."

"Well... I know she'll be alright—five cheerleaders, how much trouble can she get in, right?"

The explosion of fungalooga laughter from the five of them causes me to feel sorry for them. We are all afraid. Aren't we?

"Well, of course she can go. Just let me talk to her for a few minutes."

"Okay," Bethany Big Eyes says, accidentally giving me her *permission* to talk to my own daughter.

All six of us herd ourselves into the livingroom, where the beautiful, Italian Egyptian looking thing sits in long haired repose. Burdened by humility.

"Venicia, I'll be up in your room, honey. Okay? I'll see you in a minute."

Her smile and her nod are the company of such powerful humbleness as to be disarming, a shyness that I know better than anyone has been threatening to retreat her from the world since she was twelve years old. I turn to go up the stairs in typical Mom uselessness, powerless to effect even the ebbing of the river flow which is my daughter's life.

In the bedroom, I am struck by the notion of its sudden unfamiliarity; the growing collection of books and clocks, and the team of Barbie's that never grew past 29. The last one she bought was when she was in the eighth grade, saving the best for last, I guess, where Barbie is in the guise of an Amazon War Heroine, an Amazon Princess, who wears a gold tiara, bullet proof bracelets, and the audacity of a woman's prerogative in bright red, high heel boots, in charge of everyone of the group of classic pretties, where one bears the color of sky blue over her country checkerboard dress, carrying a picnic basket down a yellow bricked road to a city made of emerald green. The two icons stare at me without pity, nor revelation for my ignorance. They gaze at me all knowingly, so aware of what burns me up at this very moment, of what still shakes me from head to toe when I stand in front of the mirror strapped on, imagining my daughter on her knees in front of me with it down her throat in choking.

They gaze judgingly upon my perversion, upon my perverted self, as my daughter walks in tall and shapely, her big, heavy breasts seeming to call out for my attention from under her white collar shirt. As I wonder how it is possible for a woman to possess such gigantic breasts on such a small and shapely frame, I am almost ashamed, when I consider that the fear and lust I have for my own daughter is unfathomable.

I step forward through the pretense. Closing the door behind her, turning to look at her in the safety of these walls, behind the walls so filled with secrets, these walls of cultured civility, these walls of the upper room.

"What are you doing?"

"What am I supposed to do, Mom. They asked me."

"They don't give a damn about you Venicia, you know that. I know you're not that stupid."

But truthfully, the girl is only sixteen. The instinct for acceptance, the craving for the respect of her peers is as powerful as a lust in her body.

I step forward. Pushing through the last of her empty personal space. Pressing firm against her.

"What about us?"

"What *about* us," she says.

"What about *milk?*"

She laughs a quick, genuine laugh of mild shock and disbelief. The legion of dolls looks judgingly on.

"I'm not gonna do that *now.*"

"I know that. I'm just saying I don't want us to grow apart. *Milk.*"

She laughs again, shaking her head, barely able to look at me.

"Mom, you're perverted."

"I certainly am. I have a *very* perverted obsession with your well being."

"I'm talking about you and your *milk,*" she says.

"More like *you* and my milk."

She relaxes her smile away, staring at me in the look that has become so common to us over the years of her youth, as we have grown to know when the Chiming of the Nursemaids calls to fore.

"I can't now, Mom. They're waiting for me."

"I know. But if they weren't waiting."

She puts her head down, unable to fully give in to the spirit of who we are behind closed doors, with the representatives of one of the biggest high schools in Kansas in our living room.

*"There is something weird about those two."*

*"What?"*

*"They are fucking."*

*"Oh my God, you are crazy. I can't believe you said that."*

*"As sure as a strap on don't get soft, baby..."*

"Venicia, they're just using you. They're after you because you're beautiful. There's no telling what they—"

She cocks her head a bit, in a look of deep knowing, stepping away from me to her grey sports bag, then to a favorite pair of black jeans, two t shirts and two collar shirts. The big bra and tiny underwear are soon to follow. The deep burgundy of one of the t shirts and one of the button down collar shirts is regal. Soccer mom sass in solid color casual, it is. I want the burgundy for my own closet. To Hell with pastel pink, blue and beige. Her dark colors are beautiful.

"It's not *your* safety, honey, that I'm worried about."

"I'm not gonna do anything, Mom. I've outgrown that."

"So you say. But what happens if you get provoked?"

*"Venicia,"* a worried, impatient little voice calls politely from below. *"We're ready whenever you are. You want us to wait for you in the car?"*

In locked eyes, the spirit of who we are is in domain. The first two buttons of my shirt are done away with.

Deliberately.

*"I told you they were fucking, didn't I?"*

Lift me up, my darling Venicia. Slam me to the bed in grieving. In a fury uncharacteristic. To obey the ticking seconds of haste.

Her lips are clamped about my breast in vacuum suck, to pull more than the milk from the haze of slumber, to nourish a place beyond her body, to show the spirits of the dolls who judge us that they have no say, that they cannot come to life and point in warning, that they cannot indict us for what grieving we must express.

My shirt lies open. My t-shirt and bra are pulled up to my neck. The girl's strong hands are at the heavy squeeze of her desire, her lips bob up and down upon the nipple in full. Already, every pull, every sucking of what droplets come forth, every awakening of a greater stream pulls me up higher, higher from the muck of mediocrity, to raise me to the heights of glorious mountain blue, where the air is pristine, and filled with the purity of creation in power and beauty.

She holds me down in no pretense, both of us fully clothed save the one humongous breast exposed, the sixteen year old libido exploded upon the forty six year old craving, where the force and the object collide immoveable, to cause cataclysm in space time, and the irrevocable destruction and creation of forms and forces beyond explanation. She knows, as I do, to lay into the Nun's Intercourse as though there is no tomorrow, to stay upon this breast until the suffering is wrought, until the quarter is charged and given, until the debt is raised and paid in full.

I cannot close my eyes, I cannot hold them open, I cannot look away from the Amazon who indicts me without mercy, who listens to the groan escape my body through my voice long and labored, adamant and against my will. Her own breathing betrays what must happen to her in punishment, in chastisement for the unlocking of Pandora, from our partaking of the platter of fruit passed down, of knowledge from the mind of eve sent from East of Eden.

Up and down, up and down, deeply sucked in to the back of her mouth, to the front of it, until every motion of her rings a chime to my hidden breast and to my naval, then a spiral to my bowels, and to the tragedy which is the front of me, all of them meeting together as a lightning strike somewhere in the center of my body, to lift me up from the bed, pushing against her violently, amidst the dreadful appearance of a single soprano shriek from somewhere deep inside my body, sent through my voice in tragic revelation, of what secrets there are that lay buried beneath the surface of cultured civility.

*C*UNT *lickers…*

What vulgarities plague the Venicia mind! What spirit flows around her, whispering such hidden truths in her ear! As she sits in the truth or dare circle, watching two seventeen year olds tongue each other with their mouths wide open for one full minute on a dare. *What am I doing here* is another truth that torments her and will not go away, as the light now falls upon her worst fears.

"Alrightie, Miss Venicia Atwood. Showtime. First time players have to take hostess choice," Bethany says, with Brittany and Catilin glancing at each other sheepishly. "And for you, I choose…the dare."

The types of fear are many, and uniquely distinguished. Among these is the Fear of Public Humiliation, a cousin to the Fear of Pain itself.

"I will admit," she says, "we've *all* been looking forward to this honey... show us your *tits.* "

Bridgette Brown Hair, the wildest and freest spirit among them, lets out a yell and a cheer that would surely be more appropriate at a football game. But the energy from it is as contagious as a pandemic in the little room, and soon, all five girls are hooting, clapping and chanting "Nicia, Nicia, Nicia..." until she has no choice but to simply lower her head in shame and total defeat.

"Aww, come on, you can do it... Bridgette, show her how we play the game..."

Venicia looks up in time to see a pair of snow white C cups wiggling and shaking in the open air, while Bridgette twirls her neon green t-shirt over her head, with the more reserved Catilin staring wide eyed with her hands over her mouth, while Bethany leads the other two in a chorus of of clapping and screaming to the rafters. After at least 10 seconds of giving it a whirl, the girl slips back into her florescent green shirt, and the rest of the girls applaud and cheer as they would at any one of their sporting events, as Venicia must endure the third part of the truth whispered in revelation, *"God, Please help me."*

And typically, upon the heels of a prayer to be rescued, comes a slide deeper into the abyss.

"Bridgette, get that shirt back off, baby, it's your turn anyway. I *dare* you to fuck Caitlyn right in front of us."

*God, please...*

In the shock of total disbelief, Venicia watches Bridgette walk over to the Swiss blonde, Baby Spice beauty Caitlyn Stevens, and yank her hair violently, jerking her head back, pressing a deep and uncompromising kiss on her. Venicia is so entranced by the girls' bravery that she doesn't notice the clapping, whooping and hollering Bethany staring right at her.

"Caitlyn, we're gonna watch you get *fucked*. And I've got just the thing for it."

While Bethany hurries over to the closet, Venicia looks at Amber and Brittany for mercy, but to no avail. Bethany hurries back over to her pretty little puppets in waiting, the two other 16 year olds such as she, and hands Bridgette the strap on member, standing close by as she pulls it up to where her underwear used to be, helping her pull the straps tight around her big, naked hips, until the member hangs in perfect form and fashion, to that which pertaineth to a man.

"Get on your knees," Bethany orders the nervous looking Caitlyn. "Face this cock."

She turns to where the member hangs down long and lean, forward to the fullness of its phallic shape and calling. Bethany *slaps* Caitlyn just enough, then slaps her harder, telling her "you are in *so* much trouble, bitch," shaking her head on the syllable for 'so.' "Slide that cock in her mouth, Bridgette. Make her fucking choke on it."

And this, they do. As their guest looks on in rapt attention, at what things are pervasive in the hearts of girls and women.

"I said *choke* on it!"

And this, they do. As Caitlyn slides all of eight inches down her throat in epic swallowing, while Bethany holds her head there as she begins the muffled cough imprisoned by the Virgin's Intercourse, until her body begins to twitch from the gagging, her face in deep stress, until she fights to pull herself free, the member sliding all the way out and hanging down, followed by the spit and spittle that must fall, in the choking of a strand of crystalline string.

Bethany forces Caitlyn to do this at least three more times, while their guest is forced to watch by attrition, wishing that she could turn away, noticing a single, powerful twitching of Bridgette's healthy buttocks while she looks down at the Swiss blonde in the coughing, choking trauma. The shy, beautiful guest looks at Bridgette with rapt amazement, as her buttock twitches again from her standing position. The second twitch causes Bridgette to hold her head back briefly with closed eyes, saying "shit," with a touch of anger, that watching Caitlyn's suffering has brought such powerful, and premature lightning to her body.

"I need to fuck her Bethany."

"Yeah, you want to fuck her now?" she says, turning her attention to the standing Bridgette Brown Hair with the healthy hips, kissing her violently on the mouth, then giving both of Bridgette's C cups a slap and a hard, painful suck. Bethany grabs Caitlyn's head and spits in her face, telling her "turn around, you fucking slut…get on your hands and knees…now, fuck this bitch like you *mean* it."

This, they do. As Bridgette slides the member into her blonde beauty from behind, causing Caitlyn to lower her head and cry out in angry, gruff acceptance of this fate. In bitter approval, Bethany walks over to her shy, discombobulated and devastated guest, kneeling down behind her on the floor.

Suddenly, the girl's body sparks a bolt that skips her heart a beat, when Bethany grabs both her breasts from behind, squeezing them tight over her loose t-shirt, whispering *shushes* in her ear, telling her "your name is Venicia *Got Wood* at school, 'cause you give us girls a hard on whenever you come around. Now, watch Caitlyn get *fucked.*"

This, they do. With Bridgette focusing on the task at hand, holding on to the yelping, shrieking in high pitched helplessness blonde in Swiss Alpine hair, causing her to cry out in these single, high pitched yells of unseen agony from within, while Bridgette angrily slams herself into her from behind, saying exactly these words "yeah, that's right you fucking bitch, you're gonna make me cum so fucking hard you candy land *slut—*"

And upon this, an invisible bolt of energy strikes Bridgette from somewhere, shattering her rhythm, making her quickly lean forward and grab Caitlyn's bubble gum breasts, holding on to them for dear life as the lightning hits her again, causing her to spasm and yell a quick, loud woman's cry, as every muscle in her body tightens under the jiggly flesh, making her whisper loudly her favorite vulgarity "shit," the intermission between lightning strikes, as she spasms and yells a second time, still holding on to Caitlyn's breasts, whose breathing is fast, loud, and pitched in feminine suffering.

"Oh, no you don't," Bridgette says, pushing through the trauma. "Don't you quit on me, bitch. Ride that cock. *Ride it*, I said."

This, they do. As Caitlyn begins to bounce back on it in full, slamming herself back against Bridgette's body, returning to her state of high pitched helplessness, which rises her young body high and higher up, until the room around them all is filled with the death of a maiden's sanity.

$\mathcal{I}$N THE AFTERMATH of trauma. In the aftermath of grieving uncovered. She rests deeply in the arms of slumber, having been carried away from the tragedy of human existence, which is sin. But even while the images, the sights and sounds of Caitlyn's raping, the cold whisper of Bethany's mocking—even while these things were around her in her sleep, she knows that she can hardly escape judgment of herself, being a prisoner of her own fearful secret, perhaps even greater than what the teenage girls do carry.

*I know she fucked her mother, I should have asked her,* is the voice of Bethany echoing inside her mind, somewhere in the land of dreams, where she is suddenly filled with a sense of dread. Though she would like to wake up, the prospect is an impossible one, to be sure, feeling so completely drained from the night's proceeding. *Whatever ghost or demon this is, I'm going to have to fight it because I'm too tired to run,* she says in her mind, waiting fearfully for the witch to appear from the nighttime hallway, to come into the room where she lays and smother her to death. But her exhaustion is so great that she cannot move, she cannot kick or jerk herself awake in time. The presence in the room arrives to where she is, to burden her soul in fear, lifting her up and carrying her from the bed and into the hall.

*Because I said so, that's why* are the words that Bethany's voice barks into the dark around her, but somewhere just beyond her vision. *God, please let tomorrow come* is the prayer that her spirit prays, as she begins to think only of escaping from the group of girl sharks, and getting back home to her mother.

And suddenly, from within the confines of sleep, she feels the need to awaken and to draw a breath, feeling the weight of a mountain pressed down on her chest, the weight of impossibility formed. But from underneath the heavy weight pressed down, she finds a pocket of air to breathe, giving her the strength to push the heavy weight away with her mind, allowing her to draw a thick and unsatisfying gulp of hot air, to show her that yes, she is alive, somewhere just this side of the gates of Hell.

In the midst of blackness, from within the confines of a darkness that cannot be imagined, she slowly returns to sentient space in her mind and spirit, again aware that she is a corporeal being, a creature of flesh and blood, flesh which burns with a soreness from head to toe, and blood which pumps acid through her veins. She can barely open her mouth to draw in the thick, black air, suddenly aware that though she knows now that she has hands to bring up to her face, to caress the pain in her skull, that no matter how hard she tries, she cannot cause them to move. *Where are my hands,* is the tragic question which forms around her in the dark, as the answer begins to take shape and form in her mind, that her hands are bound behind her back. And she now understands that her arms are tied tight behind her back and underneath her, and that she cannot move her legs, to help her as she slowly tries to push over onto her stomach, to try and draw a glint of hope from in the midst of this blackness and despair.

In what feels like the last breath there is to breathe, she hears the trapped, terrified mouse of her own spirit begin to cry out, in a pitiful wail held in by the space around her. She grabs on to the sound of her own voice for solace, for any possibility that this can only be a dream, and that she will awaken safe and sound in her mother's arms, even at the profound comfort of her mother's bosom. But the third part of the truth is cataclysm, which descends in revelation like a funnel cloude, that she is in the confined space of a wooden box, and her hands and feet are bound, tightly enough to burn them numb with pain.

*Momma, please, please Momma help me* are the hopeless, helpless words she hears in the claustrophobic space, along with the sound of bare feet brushing against wood too dark to see. Though she tries valiantly, she cannot resist the rising tide of panic, like fools packing sandbags underneath the winds of a hurricane. She is suddenly immobile in the dark, every muscle in her body tensed, using the last of her air to elicit screams, to provide her company on this last ride to oblivion.

Then suddenly, she hears, she *feels* the wood begin to creak and pop all around her in the dark, enough to disperse the panic of her screams, soothing them down to a trickling of nervous whimpering. Then in her mind's eye, there is a vision of the ropes at her feet, which are suddenly pulled by stresses unfathomable, which she continues to see in desperation, until she hears a loud, dull popping sound like a *snap,* and the sudden freedom of movement in her legs and feet.

Amidst the last whimper is a sudden calm, enough to soothe her nerves to sanity in the dark, and cause her rapid breathing and heartbeat to subside. In her mind's eye, the stresses return to the ropes on her body, until the ropes around her stomach and bosom snap violently, the broken pieces lapping once against the inside of the darkened box. This rope vision returns with ease, taking hold of the ropes around her arms, behind her back underneath her, until the same popping sound is achieved, and the relief of pressure in every muscle in her upper body.

Then, in the heat of the calming dark, she feels the invisible hands grip the ropes at her wrists, gripping them in the tiniest space of their calling around her wrists, to make a mockery of the knots tied, ignoring them with the controlled fury of a team of oxen upon a stubborn tree stump, pulling the ropes with a strength beyond their endurance, until they snap like a tree branch under the weight of a new and heavy snow, freeing her wrists, allowing her to voice the pain of agony in her bones.

In the dark, in the pitch black, she knows to rest a moment in fetal. In preparation for the task at hand, and the returning of life giving oxygen to her body.

*I*N THE HEART of her tragic memory. Shown to her aching mind in the grieving, devastating dark, she sees Bethany Gary's smiling face, bringing her the succulent, sweet glass of orange elixir, telling her to chug the orange juice, that it was their "special drink" that they always shared together. *"But you have to chug it down,"* she says, *"just like the rest of us."* Upon the theater of her mind, she sees the lovely, white teethed Bethany Gary in full, fungalooga smile, saying *"the prettiest girl in Topeka is one of us, now."*

*"Prettiest girl in the whole damned state,"* Bridgette says, staring her up and down once from head to toe.

*"She knows that, Bridgette,"* Bethany says, in high pitched intolerance. *"Stop embarrassing her with it. Okay now, everybody lift your glasses… and by next year, the Sweet Six are gonna run this fucking school."*

Venicia is the first to turn the sweet tart elixir up to her mouth, so glad to be one of the chosen, one of the elite, the beginning of the end for the rest of the school's so called in-crowd, who will learn what it means to have social power and prestige as a teenager, from the most pathetic geek, all the way up to the ridiculous principle herself, whose days of switching her *"horse ass"* up and down the halls like the stewardess Jackie Brown are numbered. Things that Bethany and Bridgette have planned for certain individuals in that school are apocalyptic in nature.

And now, her tragic memory carries her to the darkened chambers of the upstairs hall, at the door of Bethany Gary's room. One by one, each girl gives Bethany a full, quick kiss on the lips, as they file past her to go to the guest rooms. And the beautiful, statuesque and shapely Venicia is the last to earn a kiss from the queen, feeling the spark of it light up the corners of herself, even while she has suddenly been burdened with the need for hibernation like a she-bear in September.

In the heart of this dark, upper class suburban memory, Venicia sees herself going timidly to the guest room alone, breathing in the air of modern, New World refinement and high class money well earned and well spent, with beds too elaborate to afford, and mirrored dressers too elegant and finely crafted ignore. *How can I be so lucky,* is one of the last thoughts that slips though the Kansas Country girl's mind, as she slides into the soft, plush linen, and drifts into the latter day Dream of Eve.

Then, as if in the substance of a night vision, she perceives voices that she cannot hear, motion she cannot feel, sights that she cannot see, other sounds that she cannot hear. All of this, in the swirling motion of blackness, and the feeling of the presence of *evil,* and the tightening of the blood vessels in her body, and the constriction of air from her lungs. Then from this, a space of blackness too vast, too infinite to traverse, but

but must be bypassed by the miracle of traversion through space time—from the beauty of upper class luxury and friendship of the heavenly elite, to the caustic dark inside the Gates of Hell, where every inch of skin burns with the fire of betrayal, and every breath is poisoned from the dark'ned fiery seas of regret.

From the *tranquilized* elixir, to the head throbbing resurrection, Venicia Atwood is suddenly in the tranquility of her gift, which takes hold of the fear and disperses it away, slowly expanding pressure through the small, black space around her. She pushes outward with her mind, slowly, steadily, feeling the tiny space expand again, listening to the wood creak to splitting, knowing somehow that in the totality of this potential, the creaking of this wood, the expansion of this tiny space is done without effort— which causes her to focus, holding her breath, and every muscle in her body perfectly still.

Then she pulls in the bit of air remaining, holding it in preparation for what must be, then pushes the sphere of space around her body, to expand the air outward from all around her, feeling her world grow to infinity—with her eyes closed, hearing the booming sound of *thunder* as from the clouds, missing the sight of the force grabbing hold of the wind, flashing it through the trees over where she was buried, bending them all like a gale force wind, at the heart of a thunderstorm in the twilight.

# Venicia Atwood Walks the Miles

VENICIA ATWOOD walks the miles. In the shadows of the evening day. Stumbling along the side of the country road in epic isolation. Wondering if she is still upon the earthly plane. Wandering the road from the small forest grove unfamiliar, hidden in the wide open plains of wheat. Wondering how it is possible to be on a road for so long, with not a single car passing by.

Venicia gazes up at the round, rusty light at the horizon. Hanging low above the fruited plain. The lunar light looks down upon her in mocking. With no mercy for her condition. No pity for what she feels inside and out. For the agony of aching muscle and bone. The agony of a soul's betrayal.

All she can think of is the loveliness of her mother's face. The softness of her bosom. The comfort of her soothing voice in her ear.

The swirling of the lunar light gathers about her in pain, knocking her to the ground. Holding her to the grass along the side of the road. Making it impossible for her to move.

High above the unmerciful lunar light, shines the goddess in celestial beauty. The star shines brightly above the tragedy fallen by the road. Shining above the rolling lights of earthly progression, that stop in Samaritan mercy. In pity for the lovely traveler along the road. A traveler who lies in power.

In beauty.

*I* KNOW those girls were lying.

*"We haven't seen her since last night, Ms. Atwood."* Why didn't they call the police? Why did they wait until damn near *nighttime* the next day to tell me she was missing? *"She wasn't in her bed this morning, we thought she went for a walk or something. But she never came back. We've been worried sick all day…"*

Mare Luna stares down at me in mocking. With her features dipped in pain and blood. Rising above the golden wheat field by my house, in grieving to tell me where it is that my beloved daughter could have gone. But not to ease my suffering, I think, does Luna wish to speak truth to my aching soul. No. She wishes to see me crumble under the weight of Truth itself, to see the revelation of what is, to watch it turn me into a grieving, bereaving mess of a woman. To tell me, *your daughter is a pathetic excuse for a human being...every step she takes from here to her grave is cursed.*

From the beauty of the Moon rising over the Eastern Gate, I close my eyes and try to find a place of sanity, a place where I am not tossed on a stormy sea of emotion. This, a hurricane of fear and dread, as the minutes have suddenly begun to tick away like hours, since those girls told me that they don't know where my daughter has gone. And somehow, someway, I know that there must be a balance checked; there must be a debt paid for what is owed, and I pray that Fate will have mercy on my soul, and bestow redemption and renewal to our lives.

And at the moment of truth, when I remember the impossibility of who she is and what she has done, the tiny lights of high powered flight drift toward me from high overhead, moving slowly like stars that have grown tired of their fixed place in the cosmos, and have begun their journey across the face of the earth, to decide where it is they are going to fall. If she were standing here with me now, what hope would this light over our prairie have, to make it past our horizon without bursting into flame?

Suddenly, the edge of the wheat field is lit up by the glow of white lights, appearing strangely from beside our little brick house. These are the lights of hope that beckon, calling me from the moonlit cosmos, to try and make sense of reality again. *What the Hell do you mean she's missing,* are the words I plan to speak to the Bethany Quintet, if this is them in my driveway.

But when I turn the corner from the back of the house, it is a car I have never seen before. What does this silver Intrepid intend to bring? What lost traveler within has what benign irrelevance to sing?

As I prepare to tell these strangers that no, I don't know the quickest way to get to I-40, a silhouette of raven haired beauty steps out of the passenger side, wearing her burgundy t-shirt, which barely covers her hips down to her thighs, moving towards me with outstretched arms of desperation, and a dirty, fearful expression on its beautiful face.

While the stranger in the silver Intrepid looks on, I grab hold of this beautiful thing in total disbelief, unable to understand from whenceforth it is she cometh, nor can I dismiss the feeling that this is more miraculous than her end of the world gift, and that I am seeing this girl as though she were resurrected from the grave.

# *19*

*T*HE FIVE BITCHES that are going to die, as they burden the heart and mind.

I see the death of sixteen year old Bethany Gary, who had designs upon being first among them. Being the girl in the school who is called the prettiest by attrition, whether or not it is true. Yellow blonded hair worn long and straight, blue eyes and white teeth a sparkle, the head of the junior varsity cheerleader squad already; already knowing full well that even in her junior year, she will lead the varsity cheerleaders from day one. Because her mother is a former sorority queen and surgeon, because her father is a corporate king. Because her mother is sweet with the cheerleader coaches and the lady principal. Because she lives in half million dollar luxury unbridled. Because she never receives a grade that is lower than an A. Because she drives her mother's Mercedes convertible and her father's Toyota Tundra to school, and her own Rav 4 besides. Because her mother is a graduate of Harvard Medical School and former Miss Kansas finalist, and a member of the county school board. Because the handsome boys in school have rivaled for her time and effort, and every girl has done so just the same. Because she is the darling of every teacher's roving eye, and a quiet desperation they can never come to name. Because she is a one million dollar trust fund baby two years hence, Bethany Gary is a sign of the times. Though she is a motheress from early in the game. Practiced orgasms upon her mother in private just the same. Such an end of the world secret that is too apocalyptic to name, Bethany Gary is a sign of the times.

The five bitches whom I know are going to die, as they burden the heart and the mind.

Sixteen year old Bridgette McLaughlin. Brave enough to fly among the prettiest of them. Confident enough, talented enough, bold enough to take her place at Bethany's side. Known for what is the dream and desperation of every man below the waist, hips spread to infinity. Sixteen year old curves both firm and phat, brunette beauty in kitten and kitty kat carnality. Advertising the energy she burns with inside, passed down from her blue collar waitress mother, a woman who introduced erotica to her daughter when she was eleven. Until the daughter understood early what was "The Mommy Game," filling her daughter's eyes and mind with vulgarity. An all girl erotic addiction passed down, until her daughter craves its expression in reality. Having rubbed her mother's backside at the kitchen stove, having kissed her mother upon the lips. The suggestion upon the mother's hips as to what desires must be wrought, Bridgette McLaughlin is a sign of the times. The enforcer to her mistress Bethany, having already broken a girl's finger behind closed doors at Bethany's command. In this latter day land of lasciviousness on demand, these are signs of the times.

Sixteen year old Caitlyn Stevens, daughter of a banker and his beautiful Swiss blonde wife, licked when she was a child of five by her mother's wayward tongue, these are signs of the times. A reputation in the school for deep throated fellatio, a rumor in truth passed around the school. Pale skinned, platinum blonded beauty, baby faced bubbliness and bubble gum boobs and bottom. The highest jumping, highest kicking, highest leg spreading leap of a cheerleader, out tumbling even the black girls for athletic supremacy. Adventurous on a dare, fearless to obey her mistress and her queen, the other girl laid atop the nerd girl who got her finger broken because of one smart mouthed insult too many. Having been slave to both Bethany and Bridgette for every secret depravity known. Having slapped and fought a black girl simply because it was what she was told, but singing in the glee club and a member of the Christian Fellowship of old, Caitlyn Stevens is a sign of the times.

The Five Bitches who are going to die, as they burden the heart and mind.

Amber Hall, the goody good volunteer queen, yellow blonded smiles and sweetness. Hospital volunteer, three hours a week as a curbside restaurant waitress. Taking orders and taking hearts of grown men and women, voted most likely to succeed at the end of this junior year. Kind and sweet enough to be dominated by three girls younger than she, being mysteriously alone and without a romantic other, because she was ordered by the big three to refuse every invitation, to keep herself free to do their bidding. To be free as the 12<sup>th</sup> grade liason for them next year. A girl who knows the underground truth of the Mother Lover's Society, girls who have been conquered by the mothers of their friends and acquaintances, a girl who understands that the latter day revelations are true, that there are heterosexual women hidden in the suburbs, who are predatory cougars to young kittens as prey, but this done in secret, at the home of a girl whom she babysat. When the forty seven year old woman sat beside her on the couch and said to her, *Amber, have you ever been with another woman?* When Amber was held underneath this woman on the downstairs sofa when the eleven year old girl was in the bed upstairs, when Amber Hall held the nerd girl's foot while Bridgette and Caitlyn broke her finger in private and in despair, these are signs of the times. When she heard the real estate queen ask her, *would you mind very much if I kissed you,* these are signs of the times.

And I see seventeen year old Brittany Hale, the one who works for the yearbook, the one who gives herself to poetry and reading, but whose look is too mature and sensual to be accepted by the nerd girls, her manner is to brothelly for them to embrace her without fear. The one who can rock a red dress like a hotel whore if she has too, whose Armageddon invitation came by her mother and her mother's best friend at once when she was fifteen, when she was doubly penetrated by the two of them in high rise luxury on a trip to Atlantic City. Of these impossible things I see, the girl who held the nerd girl's other foot while her finger was being broken, these are signs of the times.

Five girls graduated already from the mundanity of man. Who send violence and intimidation in private, forward and back again. When mothers burden their daughters in the depravity of lust and sin, these are signs of the times we are in.

These Five Bitches are going to die. As they burden the heart and mind.

# 20

HE TASTE of my daughter's lips are sweet as wine, and the feel of her breasts in my mouth is nourishment to my wicked soul. In the aftermath of traumas come and gone, we lay spent in my bed in the nighttime, with me laid on my back in a place where guilt cannot reach, and remorse can find no lifegiving air to breathe. My beautiful, curvy daughter lays sleepy at my bosom, her leg draped comfortably over top of mine, while her arm is laid across my stomach. I can think of nothing but her, the height and the depth, the life and breath of her, as if I too were dead, and because of her, am suddenly alive again. Gone are the days of pretense, of acting as though we are not MILF and MILFette, Mother and Motheress, and that this sixteen year old mother lover is not a killer of men, women and children.

But of what immorality is it, truly, for her to be simply who and what it is she was born to be? Who knows by what spirit her victims are being judged by, when she must reach into the space of their world, and pull them from it in fire and blood? Everything in me tried to warn me of this so-called sleep over, this ridiculous attempt at her inclusion into the flow of what is "normal." Even from the second they walked into this house yesterday afternoon, I knew that she belonged with them the same way that a baby tiger belongs with a group of full grown housecats. All I can think of is the look on those girls' faces tomorrow, when the girl they thought was dead and buried in the woods is suddenly walking the halls in front of them like a spirit resurrected.

"You're going to kill those girls, aren't you?"

The only answer she gives is a deep breath, and a more complete snuggle of her arm and leg against my body. When I close my eyes, all I can see is the silver Intrepid, with its intrepid stranger hardly waiting at all to see the reunion between me and my daughter, escaping before I had the chance to give my proper thanks, to find out who they were, where they came from, and where on earth they were going to. In my mind's eye, I can see my daughter in the evening day, running to me from the Intrepid ride, grabbing me around my body as I hug her, sliding all the way down to her knees and saying pitifully, *"they put me in the ground, Momma. They put me in the ground and I couldn't breathe..."* My daughter is on her knees in front of me, weeping me into a state of utter confusion and epic relief, as the stranger yells *"good luck,"* their hand raised in goodbye as they hurry back into the silver Intrepid, barely giving me time to yell *"thank you"* as genuinely as I can, wishing so desperately to speak to them as they slip away. But my concern now is for the beautiful girl knelt on the ground in front of me, who needs only for me to hear her as she holds me in weeping. *"They put me in the ground, Momma,"* are the words that have ensured my epic confusion, causing me to have to lift her up to her feet, and frustratedly escort her through the back door and into the kitchen, sitting her down at the table, standing up in front of her as a pillar of strength she can hold on to. *"I woke up and I was in the ground, Momma. I was tied up and couldn't see and I couldn't breathe."* And as I look closely at her hair and her oversized burgundy t-shirt stained with what looks like *dirt,* I am forced to accept that all of this insanity she speaks has its basis in reality.

*"What do you mean they put you in the GROUND,"* I say frustratedly, grabbing her beautiful, dirty face in my hands and gazing her in the eyes. *"They put you in the ground where, honey? What are you talking about?"* But she can only hold on to me tighter, as if preparing for a wave of memory, which splashes down on her like ocean surf in a storm, evoking a cry of fear from her, a wail of hopelessness and terror that chills me to the bone. All I can do is stand here and hold her tight, as she grips me around my waist, unable to speak of whatever nightmare it was she was just in. All I know is that she speaks of having been tied up in the ground, and her face and hair are corrupted with dirt. What can I do, except to bring her back from the tragedy of whatever it is that has happened. There'll be time for questions and answers later. For now, I guide the beautiful girl to the upstairs bathroom, undressing both of us, then turning the shower on in preparation.

I guide her into this crystal waterfall, joining her in this private and brief recovery, standing beside her in the shower as she lets the water drown her fears, wetting her black hair into a curtain of black, shiny silk against her ivory skin. I take up the bottle of shampoo, letting the white, liquid soap fall thickly into my hand, putting the bottle back in its place, then lathering the soap into her hair in full. Then I return her to the glory of the crystal waterfall, watching it remove the soap and invisible corruption gathered, watching her soothe her fears away in part, while I pour another thick stream of the liquid soap into my hand in awaiting. Before she can fully recover from the first rinsing, my hands are in her hair again, lathering it into a gathering of suds and soapy clean, killing the rest of what corruption hath leapt up from the ground to claim her. I stand nearby her as she rinses this death from her a second time, pressing myself close against her breast to breast, stomach to stomach, underneath the rush of falling water nearby. I take her lovely face, her perfect face into both my hands, pressing my lips to hers in full, until I feel the rest of her fear begin to leave her body. My daughter relaxes her mouth fully, returning this cause of affection, until the two of us are gathered to the heights of ecstasy in our minds, and our bodies ring the chime of the crystal waterfall, and the renewal of our hearts and souls from grieving.

# 21

*CLOSE YOUR EYES and try to sleep now*

*Close your eyes and try to dream*

*Clear your mind and do your best*

*To try and wash the palatte clean*

*You can't begin to know it*

*How much we really care*

*I hear your voice inside me*

*I see your face everywhere*

*Still, you say—*

## Venicia in the Cause of Aircraft

*We belong to the light, we belong to the thunder*

*We belong to the sound of the words, we've both fallen under*

*Whatever we deny or embrace, for worse or for better*

*We belong—we belong, we belong together*

*Pat Benatar*

*Jonathan Lovejoy*

# Venicia Atwood

# Rides the Wind

VENICIA ATWOOD rides the wind. On the eve of eschatology. Cruising the passenger seat of her mother's car, on the morning of a reckoning. The morning of a grand comeuppance overdue. Being driven in near total silence, as the mother's nerves will not let her speak. Will not allow her to speak it. Having only smiled and nodded her head at what she saw this morning, when her daughter was dressed in black. *Jet* black t-shirt and black jeans, black high heeled boots worn in leather. Married to the hair as black as a raven's feathers, around her shoulders and down the length of her back.

> *I am as boring as a sunset*
> *As dull as a starry night sky*
> *I am as quiet as the wind*
> *That causes a cloud to go passing by*

Venicia Atwood rides the wind. The wind of intentions that need not be spoken. Cruising with her mother nearby the school. Nearby the place that must serve as the benchmark. The place where her past will end, where her future must begin.

The mother is privy to the sights and sounds of wicked youth. The Rapture Generation. Young, dead souls milling about in W.A.S.P. psychology. Half rich, half grown, half dead to the illusion of morality. A thousand channels at home. A thousand dollars in gold debit to spend. A thousand years of enmity toward the Almighty matured. Grown into disinterest in him. Unable to hold the thought of him in their heads without mocking. Without resentment. Without hatred.

The girl in black leans over to her mother, and presses her lips in moaning. A lover's moan, in the wake of eyes that stare. At those who look on in fear, at who the familiar, long haired beauty might be, kissing her blonde mother smack on the lips. The beautiful girl in black turns away, gold earrings dangling, sliding out of the bluebird blue nothing on four wheels. Stepping in full, six feet of long legged, healthy hipped, heavy breasted glory. Ignoring the vulgar grimace of comic lust she sees on one of them. Not looking back at the mother, who looks after her in pity, more than fear. Looking around at the gigantic school building and property. A mental picture for a reference to compare.

Venicia Atwood rides the wind. In long legged, shapely, high heel booted step into the place of learning. The place of unlearning. Where the top ten list written on Mt. Sinai is forbidden. She steps in uneasy confidence, unable to retreat into the fullness of who they know. Into the fullness of humility. Drawing a double look from many who thought they knew her. Who thought they understood that she was pretty. But was unaware of what makeup can do to some faces. Of what otherworldly affect it can have. Only smiling at the nerd girls who wave timidly. Who wonder why she wears the thick, tough looking black belt with the big silver buckle. Wondering what purpose is the black leather armband. Wondering why her fingernails are painted black.

Venicia Atwood rides the wind. As Fate allows five pairs of eyes to step into view. Five pretty pairs of cheerleader eyes. Two varsity, three junior varsity pretties, at the edge of another summer vacation. Walking together in their core group solidified. The five of them stopping in their tracks in the hall. Unable to smile. Unable to laugh. Unable to speak.

Venicia Atwood rides the wind. On the morning of this day of reckoning. Suddenly getting up when the class bell rings. Not looking at the three of them in the eye. Turning to the teacher with a dismissive smile, and a half whispered word mouthed: *"emergency."* Turning near the last moment to the Bethany girl. Staring at her in the eyes. Then at the last moment, before the door closes, running her hand across her own throat. The universal sign. Meant to cause one of the many fears. The one that is most powerful. The most tragic to endure.

Venicia Atwood rides the wind. On the eve of eschatology. Stepping through the halls of learning. The halls of unlearning. Her mind already lifted upon gentle breezes. Drifting through space and time.

She opens the door into the eve of summer. Into the warm, Kansas morning. Not bothering to look up, as she walks into the open field nearby the school. The place where the young and old play the fool. Surrounded by the green grass. And the scattering of trees nearby.

She focuses her gaze upon the school. Feeling the lust of the flesh. The lust of the eyes. The pride of life. Perceiving the giddiness of Hope.

The ignorance of today. The tragic naiveté of tomorrow. The fullness of every sinful heart. The cold emptiness of every soul.

A tugging from above draws a breath deep into her body. Closing her eyes to the green landscape, to the whispering message in the nearby trees.

Venicia Atwood rides the wind. Feeling a lightness in her mind and body. A lightness that trains her gaze upward. Up and upward high above, to the great looking away, to the spirit of the Great Beyond. To the glint of silver judgment adrift.

She turns to walk further away. Deeper into the morning field of dreams. Where no such disturbance of prying eyes may stare. Before the arrival of their foolishness. Their blind stupidity. Their hopeless longing.

Venicia Atwood rides the wind. The winds of jet streams gathered and dispersed. Invisible forces done away with, gathered up and reformed. To grip 250 souls in sorrow. To make them understand the nature of fear. The nature of pain. The Fear of Death. The Fear of Hell.

The winds of warning carry a message of thunder and fire. Fire spat from the wings of silver technology. Plummeting in diagonal course toward the ground.

The beautiful girl in black gazes upward. Surrounded by a curtain of air in expansion. Waving her hair as a silken, midnight cloth in the summer wind. She stares upward into the morning sky. Watching the truth descend in silver, moving faster and faster toward the earth. She watches the tiny silver object grow larger. Taking the shape of a mechanical bird in flight. Speeding in diagonal form and direction, pointed downward towards its destination. Announcing its presence in screaming thunder. The voice of impending tragedy. Of future devastation unleashed.

The death arrow flies in silver pointed wing. In lightning and screaming thunder toward the ground. Carried on a stream of energy unseen. Of divine retribution unbridled.

The girl in black watches the Great Silver Arrow crash into the ground. Exploding a cloud of liquid fire across every brick and fleck shard of glass from the school. Bursting every remaining piece of stone and paper into flame. Sending a thousand souls burning to the hereafter. To the place where the fire burns a liquid flame. Outer darkness, in weeping and gnashing of teeth. Burning blue and black fire.

Venicia Atwood rides the wind. On the eve of eschatology.

# The Best of

# Both Worlds

# 23

THE BILLOWING CLOUD of inky black smoke rises from the red and orange flames in the Kansas morning. I had barely made it back to the house. Barely turned the television on. Before the revelation of premonition came forth. Before the world saw the Airline Graveyard take the 35th air tragedy in the last 10 years. I am unique among those who watch this tragedy on the news, as I do so with a sigh of melancholy relief. The kind that comes after the doctor's visit has ended, and whatever torture they have devised is over. An itchy groin and a visit to the drug store is preferable to being propped up on a table with my legs spread open, while a lady pervert licensed and trained to molest other women in the name of medicine goes digging around between my legs, to satisfy a lust so deep that it drove her through 10 years of education too difficult to imagine.

I breathe this similar sigh of relief, that my epic expectations are finally over, when I see the flames and the devastated Topeka High School, and the caption that tells of over one thousand souls departed. Over two hundred fifty passengers and over seven hundred students, every classroom filled to the morning brim. I must be the only person on earth who sees this, who breathes easier in the cause of it, who breathes easier in spite of it, and because it has finally come and gone.

Oh, Lord, why must thou tarry in thy coming! What greater and more terrifying things must come upon this earth!

I turn the television off again, walking back out into the morning sunlight, strangely at ease with this impending journey. It has been said that a person has to be who she is—you cannot break the mold. All attempts to do so are futile. Every human being east of Eden is subject to this, is a prisoner of the collective dark destiny which is human history— where so-called good people are the victims of bad things, or are the perpetrators of the unspeakable. *Nice people killed Christ,* is the truth that whispers itself to me, as I am reminded that there are none who are good. If there were, then what would be the point of Redemption, or the existence of the train to Hell, and the appearance of every human soul upon it, and its designated journey to the Lake of Fire and Brimstone? Since the exile from the Garden, where the door to Paradise is guarded by a flaming sword, evils have been given predestined paths into reality, every one of those being through the hearts and minds of women and men. Our victimization of one another is a two way street. It is the tragedy of human existence, which is Fate, or what is meant to be. It is that thing that puts a preacher behind bars for killing his wife—it is the thing that puts a frigid Christian wife in the bed of her next door neighbor while her husband is at home on the computer typing up something for his job, whatever it is, and in grieving to figure out how to be an emotional refuge for his wife. It is the thing that drives a community minded, church going do-gooder to build a crawlspace under his nice little brick home, where the bodies of dozens of his dead victims are buried. It is the thing that drives a talented young artist who has success in the military, to set himself up in a position to order the extermination of at least 6 million people; it is the same thing that causes a country in need of labour for their cash crop fields, a crop that colors the fields as white as new fallen snow—it is this same spirit that calls these land owners to kidnap and enslave millions of people through generations of animalistic treatment—it is all of these things, and the echoes of them in microcosm, that reveal the hearts of humanity exposed, the minds of Adam and Eve passed down, to show the need for Redemption from one individual to the other. Of what need is it to judge one another's private sins, on the eve of the Second Coming? There are *none* who are good, all are instruments and agents of the same evil, and God chooses the vessels through which his righteous judgments are brought forth. There is the need for another Ark pending, this one, to bring the judgment sea of liquid flame, where the elements will melt with fervent heat, in the rain of fire and brimstone from Heaven.

The fire and smoke I see were done little justice on the television screen, somewhere beyond the line of traffic on this road to the school, and the confusion of policemen and their determined looks of robotic importance. Oh, thou wicked and perverse generation, how can ye escape damnation! Of what authority does one man or woman have over another, accept what jobs and man's laws dictate! What job and earthly authority will earn them a trip through the pearly gates!

I park my SUV, which is the color of bluebirds, off the side of the road, well before arriving to where the policeman is diverting traffic. I can see clearly the open space of the school yard across the road, beyond the news vans and police cars and desperate parents waiting for their brains to process the truth. There is nothing for me to do but walk down this road in W.A.S.P. authority, gold earrings and gold hair in place, teal cardigan hung hopelessly over what mountains the teal t-shirt can hardly hide. I thank God for my small waist as I walk, which keeps me from being called fat by every other woman who might glance at my bosom. And as to the tragedy packed into my jeans, I always try to hide in long t-shirts and sweaters that hide the hourglass truth, which makes me feel like a stuffed sausage sometimes, or like one of those fertility statues where some headless woman has a pair of Vesuvian thighs to go with her Olympian breasts. How these pinup models have the courage to show their bodies on camera is beyond me, as I barely even have the courage to show it to my own daughter, though her own curves are clearly the origin of my own. Though she is kind, I know my breasts and hips are *way* too big to go unnoticed, so I do struggle to keep them concealed as much as I can.

In pear hipped, round breasted glory, I walk down the road, which is several hundred yards away from the burning school, until I see my way clear to turn down the tree lined street that can take me closer to this tragedy. From this street, I cross over to where I can see the fence surrounding the athletic field, which seems completely abandoned, as everyone is so focused on the busy, traffic filled road that runs past the front of the school. This view of the tragedy is pristine and undisturbed, probably because it is just too far away for anyone to relax and stay out here. Otherwise there would be a sea of cameras and reporters and desperate parents looking on. I start my instinctual walk, through the fence onto the school property, hardly able to stay focused on the burning tragedy, surveying the huge green field and groves of trees nearby the school, circling around away from the football field to the open meadow of grass and trees.

There is nothing left of the airplane that crashed, save a scattered field of burning debris where the school once was, the whole scene looking as though the plane crashed into the main school building and blew it into a billion burning fragments of a building. I walk through this open field behind the school, looking around with perfect knowledge of forethought, until I see something that makes me lower my head in tragic acceptance of what must be. Breathing a busty teal, cashmere sigh, I walk closer and closer to the lone figure standing a great distance away from the smoke and fire. The beautiful girl turns to look at me, shocked to see the busty, hippy blonde woman which is her mother in a hip length, open cashmere sweater and jeans, walking up to her without judgment, nor the slightest bit of resentment or onlooker's pity. Whatever scolding or lecture, or evil eye she expected is replaced in her vision with a look she cannot turn away from, nor can she easily process or understand. It is a look of profound understanding. A determined, direct assault on the bullshit of emotional betrayal, and judgmental delusions of morality.

I stand between my daughter and this fiery tragedy. Staring at her until she understands that between us, there are no barriers. That there is one place in the world for her to go, where she knows that she can rest. Where she knows that she will not be betrayed.

Nearby the chaos of smoke and sirens, I lean against my daughter. Hugging her tight around her waist and her back. Leaning my head on her shoulder in comfort and grieving.

# 24

$\mathcal{M}$Y MOTHER belt whipped me until I was twenty one years old. And these were not quiet, controlled little sessions over the jeans, that might leave me with a warm reminder or two of what negativity is. These were naked or underwear clad beatings, *"old fashioned, dying killings"* she used to call them, that were accompanied by abject humiliation and tears, as I never developed a tolerance to the pain. After my father died when I was sixteen, the whippings she had always craved on me just got worse, as I used to wonder if I was the only girl in school who was belt whipped to bruises and blood by her own mother. The whipping would go on and on and on, well past exhaustion, well past my ability to hold back the tears, until it felt like my entire body was on fire. And sometimes the punishments did not end there, which I would not know at the beginning would happen or not.

I was raised on a small farm in this very state, where my mother and father were typically religious, but through atypical fanaticism. I was raised by people who believed that abstinence was next to Godliness, and that it is holiness or it is Hell. My mother never wore pants a day in her life that I remember, nor did she strike a lick of makeup on her beautiful face. Even in church, she could hardly hide the innate sensuality, like Marilyn Monroe in that horse movie with Clark Gable, where an unnaturally pretty woman tries too hard to look country and plain, but failing miserably in the process.

Caroline Bourbon was all curves and all smiles in public, but no tolerance and no nonsense behind closed doors, as I was worked on throughout my childhood, until it was something that I well understood. *"I'm gon' give it to you like my Momma gave it to me this time,"* she would say, when she wanted me to know the depth of what I was going to have to go through. Caroline Bourbon had no outlet for whatever it was that was burning her up inside, except these punishment sessions done with me, which so often whirled into what I'm sure no one in her church would have believed or understood.

Sixteen is the door to a woman's future. This is true from family to family, from mother to daughter in generations around the world passed down. For me, it is but a few days after my father's funeral, when I was not in the mood for her Cinderella meddling into my free time after school.

*"I'm doing my schoolwork,"* I had snapped at her. *"God, if you would just wash your own dishes."* And suddenly I hear a fast, heavy walk up from the bottom of the wooden stairs, footsteps with purpose, echoing their way from the stairs, down the hall and into my room.

*"What did you say to me?"*

The types of fear are many. And uniquely distinguished.

*"All I said was I was doing my homework."*

*"And then you took God's name in vain, and you called me a name I will not repeat."*

"Momma, *I did not, I would never say anything like that."*

But in a glee rarely seen in moments of such bitterness, she grabs my sixteen year old baby fat face in both her hands and says, from somewhere deep within, *"you said 'goddammit, if only you weren't such a bitch,' I heard you as plain as the nose on your fat face."*

*"Momma I swear to God I didn't say that, I swear I didn't."*

*"And now you're gonna add lying and blasphemy to it."*

*"I'm not lyin' Momma. All I said was—"*

*"Shut up! Shut your lying, blasphemous little mouth. You think just because your daddy died you can disrespect me now and get away with it?"*

In the madness of new rage born, she straddles me in my homework chair. Nearly pressing her lips against mine while she speaks.

*"You think just because you've got a fat little ass and big tits now that you can disrespect me and get away with it? I'm gonna show you what you can get away with. I'll teach you to call me a bitch. I'll teach you to take God's name in vain."*

*"But I didn't."*

The tear that falls does so in vain, as she stands up and tells me to undress. And this, I do in fear, having never been able to handle the burning of the belt on my skin.

*"Lay your ass on that bed. Put your hands underneath you between your legs."*

I do what I can to comply. Having no earthly idea that she can possibly mean what it sounds like. But in the next instant, she does the impossible, and I feel the tops of my thighs at my buttocks being spread wide open.

*"I said put your rebellious hands on it! You're old enough to call me a bitch you're old enough to know where to put your hands."*

And this, I do. Pressing my fingers to the front of it underneath me. In their proper place. Their improper place.

*"Now turn your face to the wall."*

The next several minutes are filled with the sounds of opening doors and drawers, tinkling buckles and sliding fabric, joined by the feel of her fingers at my ankles, and the sound of stocking fabric being tied into a knot around them. Any hopes I may have had of getting up from this bed have just ended.

*"Turn your face to me."*

And when I do, I am privy to what the Bible was trying to say, when it said that it is a shame to speak of those things which are done of them in secret.

*"Momma I swear I didn't— "*

*"Shut up!"* She says it sharply, full of rage, holding the belt firm in one hand, standing nude and as shapely as a naked Jennifer Lopez used to be, with two of the longest, heaviest watermelon breasts hung down, to contrast the strapped on member hanging down from between her legs in full, faux phallic glory. *"You shut your lying mouth or I swear to God and Jesus I will put it down your throat…"*

All I can do is stifle the next *"please,"* staring wide eyed at the thing she wears hanging down, a mule-dicked momma if there ever was one, to make me understand the power of the Fear of Rape.

In the next moment, I see this fit waisted woman with the big hips stand up Amazonian and straight, the best of both worlds coalesced into one magnificent form. *"Turn your face to the wall."* And this, I do. Feeling the air in the room change its shape in space time, to accommodate a powerful movement of energy created, feeling a flame of fire lick the skin on my backside. I let out a yelp, but more from fear than the pain, knowing instinctively that I had better keep my mouth shut on the second one.

Sometimes, a sadist wants to cause injury in silence. Then, the sound of her victim's voice is a distraction, rather than a delicacy.

The second blow, the third, the fifth, the seventh, the ninth and beyond stripe lines of fire through the skin of my backside, as I hold my hands between my legs, wondering how many more I will be able to take, before my voice cries out on its own. Five. Four. Three. Two…

The last one is created on top of the one before it, and I hear the scream come out through a straining to prevent it. It infuriates her, I know, as the next three blows come in a flurry, with me having to scream fully now, and begin to move my buttocks around for relief.

*"Stop moving and shut up. If you move again, or if you make another sound I'll put the next one in the middle of your back. Rebellious… little… slut."*

The last syllable brings forth the feel of another fire brand to my hips, causing me to have to bury my face in the bed linen beneath me and let out another strained scream, muffled into the mattress. Whether or not this last, muffled scream has angered her, I do not know. I only know that I hear the tinkle of the belt buckle as it falls to the floor, then I feel the weight of her climbing onto the bed.

What comfort, or discomfort is this impending? Either way, I feel hope descending with her hands, sliding down my back and across my burning buttocks, fumbling at the center of them, spreading them open, dropping spit generously onto my rectum.

*"Keep your hands between your legs,"* she says, her voice noticeably deeper and more quietly determined. Then, in the same instant, my body twitches a spark of fear, when I feel the tip of the impossibly large head of the realistic member, pressed in pushing into my bottom. There is no quieting of the voice of this scream that must be, no threat with the power to subside it. This, she knows, as she lies down and wraps one strong hand fully around my mouth, while gliding her member halfway into me with the other.

The air in the room vibrates with the sound of a muffled scream, a scream held prisoner by the hand of another.

She holds her hand over my mouth, pressing herself heavier down upon me, squeezing her massive hips one last time, sliding every inch of herself deep up inside me, then laying there full upon me, breathing into my ear without ceasing. Listening to me scream. Deep, hoarse screams from pure agony, as I feel this truth take its place in my body, burning blue and black fire.

She holds me there. Waiting until my weeping subsides. Absorbing what hope I have left into her mind and body.

*"Rub yourself good,"* she says. *"Until I tell you to stop."*

This, I do. Knowing better than to pretend I don't know what. She squeezes herself onto me again, as if it is an involuntary motion slowly unleashed, her breath shuddering lightly into my ear. *"Touch yourself good,"* she breathes, her voice deep with a suffering beyond understanding—a pain too deep to comprehend. *"Squeeze your hips"* she says. *"Rub yourself."*

This, I do. But not to her satisfaction. Unable to fully comply. Not knowing that there are tracks laid for us in life that will be traversed. Directions that will be taken.

In the midst of her own suffering, she places her hands inside where mine were a moment before. Moving mine away. Memorizing the front of me, while the member is pushed all the way into my bottom. Causing my body to respond to the new stimuli. Making me understand the depth of feeling. The third part of the truth exposed. The twinge and twang of a pleasure forbidden.

The feel of her hands at my groin runs a loop through my body. From my groin, up to both my breasts, to the fire in my bowels. The pain inside my bottom is transformed to the impossible. To a feeling of pleasure morphed to ecstasy in my lower body. A pleasure radiating from my bowels to her fingers at my groin, to both my breasts mashed against the bed.

As if by her body's instinct unknown, she pushes herself into me again. A motion that strikes a spark from the open flame. To ignite a fuse towards devastation. A sparkling trail to eschatology.

When she pushes in again, my breathing takes on a life of its own. To protect my body from the trauma. To protect my mind from devastation. To protect my sanity.

Underneath her, my body rises to a trembling. A quaking of spasms uncaptured. Erupting through my voice in siren. A soprano of suffering.

Above me, I hear the words *"Oh God and Holy Jesus"* spoken in fear. In hopeless longing. A feeble prayer for a reprieve.

This prayer goes unanswered, as her body begins a steady, powerful tremble. A quaking that envelops her from head to toe. A place where breathing is not possible. A vacuum of trauma done in and around her body. Then, I hear Fate have mercy upon her life, granting her a breath. A single breath to save her life.

Allowing her to scream.

# 25

MY DAUGHTER'S BREASTS are my desperation. Two big, long and beautiful things they are, hung low and rounded above her waist, so that when she is naked, the effect is extraordinary to behold. These are passed down through the generations of her, the length and flop from my mother, and the sheer size of them from me, though I think that they have not seen the last of their growth. At sixteen, she is a breast prodigy, if there is such a thing, which made her the envy and desire of every condemned human being in that school, man, woman, boy and girl alike—Venicia Atwood was ridiculed and worshipped for the size of her tits.

It is a mother's secret revealed, here at the end of the age, that the taste of her breasts is as powdered confection upon my palette, and the feel of her nipple pulled deep into my mouth is nourishment for my soul.

*"I want to do something special with you when I get home,"* I had said, standing in the open field by the school, between her and the end of the world disaster she caused. And I can remember marveling at the timid, humble look that colored her expression with innocence, which only made me more determined to use her for my own perverted pleasure when we got home. After all, it's the least of what she deserves, right? Wrong. As Clint Eastwood prophesied in *Unforgiven: "Deserve's got nothin' to do with it."* It's just the simple truth that I am a perverted bitch behind closed doors, and my greatest desire is to fuck my daughter up the ass.

What is the mind of Eve passed down? What is the darkest dream east of Eden? The long, thin member I have already achieved. Bought at the Adam and Eve store but a few weeks ago, when I had already made up in my mind that the time had come. The time to take her anal virginity without mercy. As I had mine taken from me. But is that why I am going to do it? Is that the excuse I give myself—the fortress of blame I hide behind? Is that what the psychiatrist would say if I told them the truth, that it is a *"latent desire born from your own teenage experience with your mother?"* Whatever. All I know is that I am going to use my penis envy to my body's advantage sometime between now and the fall of night, as the world turns toward the evening day.

The sunset over the prairie looms over our western horizon. The sun rests big and orange over the great open plain of wheat. The great disk of the sun is colored in orange crimson, to echo any given sunset over the battlefields of Armageddon.

"I'm never going back to school again," she says. "I don't care anymore what happens to me."

"Well, I *do* care. I do care. It's my job to care. And as long as I'm alive, you will have a place to live. And food to eat."

"You gonna let me hang around here and do nothing? Mooch off you for the rest of my life?"

"You're only sixteen. You don't know what you're going to do yet."

"Yes, I do."

"So do I," I say, standing up from the patio chair, walking over to her and whacking her hard on the bottom.

"God," she says, genuinely shocked. "You're worse than a *man.*"

"You better believe it, baby. I told you, we're gonna do something special, and you're not getting out of it."

Again, I see the flash of innocence touch her expression.

"Come with me. There'll be plenty of time for sunsets later."

I take my daughter by the hand, leading her through our isolation into the house, as though leading the lamb to her proverbial slaughter, as the sun drifts toward the western gate. I have my hand firmly in place on her backside as we walk, slipping her a perverted and private peck on the cheek at the foot of the stairs, taking one last taste of innocence before it is spoiled fruit from the forbidden tree.

"You act like we've never done this bef—"

"Shh."

I shush her gently, my finger in place over her full lips, this finger soon replaced by my own lips at hers, moving in for the kill, kissing her deeply with or without her full consent, then moving the kiss to her cheeks, her nose, her eyes, her ears, then down to her neck, where my horny tongue takes its part in ice cream licking, licks dried by lips at the places where my tongue hath been. From the sides of her long, pretty neck, up to her cheeks again, I turn to where her lips and tongue wait to be teased, tested and tasted again by my depravity. In a lust too depraved to fathom, I take my daughter's black shirt off, my astonishment renewed once again, at the sheer size of this girl's breasts on a body so fit and normal. Even in the F cup black bra, her cleavage aspires toward the Gee Whiz, toward the key of G Major. On a body her size, breasts like these are of legendary heft and substance to behold.

Still fully clothed, I slide one of her gargantuans out, pulling the great, dark areola into my mouth for a full, deep sucking, where there is no quiet kissing, but a noisy nursing of the nipple in full, suckling repose. I release it once in that loud, popping sound, causing her breath to shudder, as I return to this devastation for at least another minute. Finally, I must raise up from the irresistibility of the nipple, to that of her lips again— backing away in full blown erotic heat unbridled, unbuttoning my shirt while I stare at the single breast exposed, flopped over the black bra fabric pulled down. I am compelled to slide and toss my shirt away, kicking out of my shoes, then making quick work of the jeans until they seem to vanish to another place, then reaching back to undo my bra, a motion that my daughter's body responds to, as I notice her exposed nipple begin to grow harder on its own. Finally, I slide my huge buttocks free from their cloth prison, my great, white breasts hung heavy as I bend over to slide the tight underwear down and away.

"Wait right here," I say, going to the closet—where all such instruments of behind closed doors death seem to lie hidden—removing the thing upon the leather harness, in the shape and form of that which pertaineth to a man.

"Oh, my God," she says, looking away, holding her hands over her mouth. She looks back at me as I slide into the tangle of leather straps, her hand still over her mouth, unable to speak the name of the Almighty again, lest he betray and abandon her.

In full, wide hipped, strapped on nudity, I walk back over to the stunned girl, sliding her pants away, after the boots are come and gone, then fully exposing those big floppers, tossing the bra somewhere unknown. I stand this shapely, statuesque young girl in a grown woman's body in front of the mirror, giving her underwear clad bottom the whack of its life with the palm of my hand, staring at her in the eyes, my own expression burdened by frustration and melancholy.

"Take your underwear off," I say, which I watch her do with great interest, to enjoy the sight of her big bosoms dangling a bell chime heard from here to our lonely horizon, as the sun disappears beyond the Western Gate.

The lotion squeezed upon my middle finger is the call sign to this diversion. She watches with great interest, standing breasty and bare, as I begin the end of her days, sliding the finger up into her rectum, watching her tense up, her beautiful face twisted in mild discomfort. I hold it in as deep as I can, watching her breathe, watching her face relax, feeling her body relax from the outside in. I reach down, to one of the great hanging breasts, pulling it deep into my mouth, feeling her body tense up on its own, hearing her whisper "Oh my God," as her expression returns to discomfort.

As to the feeling which spasms the twitches through her body, she does not know. I stand up straight, pressing my other hand to the front of her, to memorize it at the proper place, watching the big breasted girl in the reflection look down in epic anguish and disbelief. But of this, I dare not move, feeling the great swelling of the front of her in my hand, the lubrication of it, and the warning that it is now a danger to her body's stamina and equilibrium. I need only move my lips in the vicinity of hers, before she is upon them in an epic kiss, of a fever unfamiliar, and a desperation previously unknown.

But it is time.

I move my kiss away without mercy, stepping behind her, while she looks at her already devastated self in the mirror. And in keeping with this path already chosen, I observe her expression turn to apocalyptic shock, as I slide the head of this fire into her backside, slowly, carefully and completely, as she leans onto the dresser with both hands, her eyes closed, teeth grimaced in an un-smile for the ages, struggling to hold herself steady against the threshold of pain about to be breached.

"Put your hand between your legs," I say. "Relax and breathe." This, she does. Taking long, deep breaths in desperation, causing her heavy bosom to rise and fall, while both her hands are tucked tightly between her legs. I grab hold of her, pinning both her arms, preparing her for the final push. Without a word, I slide the rest of this fire deep up inside her, amazed at the power of the deep, woman's scream that erupts from her body.

I hold her there. Watching her lower her head and yell once more, but with half the power and strength of before. From behind her, the feel of my own nipples against her back very nearly has their premature effect on me, causing me to steady myself in perfect stillness, lest the room begin to haze around me and the next scream I hear is definitely my own. I slide my hands underneath her arms to her bosom, and begin to pinch and tweak both nipples in determined rhythm, causing the discomfort and shock to return to her expression, as she repeats *oh my God oh my God* with increasing anguish and severity.

As to the power of what threatens her epic destruction, she does not know. She only knows that every motion of the nipples sends her closer to the edge of stability, a place higher then where she has ever known, further than where she has ever been. By instinct, born from I know not where, I go faster upon her nipples, hearing the third syllable in her *oh my God* go up to a quick siren, watching her push back onto the fire inside, until even the first syllable of her prayer is transformed to a high pitched and pitiful wailing, sung loud and strong into the space around us, while I grip hold of her tightly to steady the both of us, as I ride the waves of both our body's spasms into oblivion.

# A Sequoia Among Pines

# 26

THE YEARS pass over our grief and sorrow, moving us from one place along the timeline to the other. The world has very nearly forgotten the cause of aircraft over Topeka, and the tragedy of over 4000 souls who have come and gone. What anomaly in the Earth's gravitational field, they ask, what of electromagnetic this and that, what terrorist ingenuity struck on these 39 flights has gone unclaimed, undetected and undiscovered, why was God mad with Topeka and not Las Vegas, Nevada? Regardless, the world breathes its collected sigh of complacent relief, after the Thirty Nine Flights of Topeka have passed into history and lore.

These eleven years have seen the growth of a sequoia among pines. Tucked away in isolation, where the rest of the world is not privy to its existence, and therefore can take no measuring stick to the base of its glory.

Venicia Marianna Atwood is beyond beautiful. It is a radiance unnatural, an elegance of loveliness unheard of, an expression of sensual purity unseen. The paleness of her skin has deepened to a rich, golden fairness of Mediterranean slant, as a snow white W.A.S.P. might hope to achieve from days in the tropical rays of sunlight. Her hair is still as black as a raven's feathers, laid about her shoulders and down the length of her back. Her eyes are as black as pools of midnight oil, and as hypnotic as an Egyptian Queen of the Gods. The nature of her unclothed body can only be seen to be imagined or believed; it is truly a work of divine art, where every fleshy curve, crease and crevice are all an extension of feminine beauty undaunted and displayed as an endtime warning from God.

It has been seven years since she has left this farm for anything other than a ride, or long distance vacation in seclusion, where those who catch an unguarded glimpse of her do so at the brief detriment of their sanity. There is a magic in her appearance that goes beyond the vague emptiness of the world, to conjure the idea of what is necromantic to consider. I have watched actresses and beauty pageant queens closely for many years since I began to notice my daughter's transformation, and whether or not I am biased may be immaterial, as I am forced to conclude that Venicia Atwood is probably the most physically beautiful woman in the world.

But that is neither here nor there, I suppose, especially when spoken by the mother of the redwood woman in question. She is at her favorite place in back, at her favorite time of the day, when the world has turned to deep twilight, nearby the edge of night. When the winter skies have come and gone, and the wheat fields around us are again golden in the summer breeze, I look forward to my brief time away from LMN on my big screen TV, and a stroll out onto the open Kansas prairie with my daughter. Sometimes we will walk the length of the great open space, until we find a lonely grove of trees beyond one of the horizons, where we will enjoy the shade or the shameful in secret, depending on what mood strikes us and when. But more often than not, it is merely a stroll to an earthly paradise, far away from the prying eyes of a condemned hoarde, and whatever judgments of ugliness or beauty they bring. She has enjoyed a natural healing from the traumas of her youth, and the tragedy of human existence, which is sin. We languish here together, the two of us, safe from what latter day tragedies must befall them in their cities and suburbs, to commune with the wonders of nature, and the open spaces of redemption and renewal.

I see her afar off, barely able to perceive her silhouette among the twilight grain. If she were any further away, she would be completely invisible in the coming dark. One hundred, two hundred yards, I don't know. How do people know automatically how many feet or yards or miles away something is? I never have.

The glory of a shooting star captures my attention. Trailing into a tiny, bright burst of sparks high overhead. I know that she saw it the same as I, and I know now that it could be another hour before she comes in. There's probably no need to shine my little Maglite at her, just to get no answer from hers. I've never seen anyone so completely disposed to lonerism, other than myself, but even I have to go into town sometimes just to see and be seen. There are times when I would have liked to drag her to Walmart or Target, in grieving to make all the other W.A.S.P. mothers so jealous that I can see it on their faces when their arrogant little self important smiles disappear.

No, she's not an actress. No, she's not a model. And yes, she is my daughter. Look at my daughter's breasts. Look at my daughter's ass. Does she make your daughter look like a popsicle stick turned to the side? A lollipop head on a stick? A Buddah Girl? A troll? What does your daughter look like compared to mine? Is your nerd at Harvard? Princeton? Yale? Does your little poster child for Anorexia Nervosa compete in local beauty pageants? Does she goalie in soccer? Does she rush the volleyball net? Is your daughter a lesbian? How progressive.

The glory of another falling star captivates my attention. This must be a meteor shower she knows about. There's no wonder she's out in the middle of the field. Far away from the lights of my feeble earthly progression. Before long, I see the flash of another bright meteor, immediately followed by a third. A fourth. A fifth. A sixth and…

The seventh meteor is lost in a simultaneous glow of sparks appearing all over the sky, down toward the western horizon. It is truly a magnificent thing to…

Oh, God.

$\mathcal{I}$N OUR NIGHTTIME KITCHEN of dreams, the beautiful young woman prepares her favorite cooking feast. Milling around the kitchen, pulling tomatoes and lettuce and cheeses from their cool, dark hiding place, to cut and grate them for her own hungry pleasure. The tender, seasoned ground beef rests neglected on the white stove but for the moment. In the adjoining living room, I am compelled to firmly say what is on my mind, turning the volume on Michelle Pfeiffer and Harrison Ford's ghostly prophecy down just enough. So as not to miss Harrison's underwater comeuppance overdue.

"Honey, whatever it is you're thinking about doing, I'm asking you to please don't."

"I'm just eating dinner, Mom. As usual, what are you talking about?"

I watch the girl in the tight, tiny black Hanes underwear cloth, the jet black briefs and matching sports bra, both pulled so tight in the midst of their calling. Her cleavage moves while she grates the orange and white cheddar into a bowl. Her soft taco shells are in the oven.

"Please don't make me say it, honey. We don't have secrets."

"Mom, I *really* don't know what you're talking about."

As she works the cheddar across the silver grate, I see in her a determination to keep away from this secret thing she plans, this impossible thing she must consider. She is so completely set on this path that she could care less if I can see her deception. In her behavior is a quiet, determined dare, a challenge to me, to even think of affecting whatever apocalyptic decision it is she has made.

But I am still her mother.

I stand up in defiance to her grown up resistance, in defiance to her rebellion, walking over to the counter where she is hungrily at work, taking a seat on one of the black counter stools. Tasting a shred of the Vermont white cheddar. Some foods are a bolt of lightning to the palette.

"That was a pretty intense meteor shower, wasn't it?"

"What meteor shower?"

I stare at the beautiful, underwear clad cook. Watching her begin to squirm. She tucks her lips, turning to the soft shells waiting in the oven. Their scent is a call to a hungry mind, body and soul. When she turns back to the counter, I stand up and walk around the corner into the kitchen. Standing close behind her. When she picks up the tomato killing blade, I gently, firmly place my hand to her wrist. Holding it tight.

"It took me ten years to get where I am with you. To get to a place where I wasn't scared to death of the sight of you. And I swear to Almighty God and Jesus... you'll have to *kill* me to make me go back. So I'm asking you again Venicia... what was that meteor shower called?"

She puts the knife harmlessly on the counter, standing with her head lowered. Staring at the blade.

"It didn't have a name," she says. "It wasn't a regular meteor shower."

My pressing against her shifts ever so slightly. To a greater completion.

Oh, what delusion is motherhood! What illusion is a mother's hold on her daughter!

"Turn around. Look at me."

The dejected, hopeless look on her face very nearly causes pity.

Nearly.

"I can't help it," she says. "I'm not hurting anybody."

"But what are you planning?"

"I'm not planning anything Momma, I swear..."

"Because Venicia, if I thought for one second that you were—"

"I'm *not*," her voice cracking on the syllable. When she blinks her lovely eyes, the tear takes hold of my compassion, drawing me into her busty and healthy hipped space of being. A hug from her still chimes my body's bells to ring.

"Don't you *ever* hold back another secret like that from me, do you understand?"

She nods her head pitifully, sniffing, her beautiful face made more beautiful by the Ugly Cry.

"Venicia...if I have to, I will still punish you. You know that, don't you?"

"Yes, Momma."

I touch the side of her face in reassurance. In what comfort I am allowed to give her at this moment.

"Kiss me," I say. This, she does. Kissing me full on the lips, in the place where all of our pretense went to die so many years ago. The kiss causes me to have to take the loudest, deepest breath through my nose, literally drinking the taste of my daughter's lips.

"Go over to the couch," I say, in what breath I have left to breathe.

"Yes, Momma."

I watch this exquisite young woman walk her underwear hips over to the sofa and sit down. In compliance. Obedience to her mother's will. As I walk slowly to the living room after her, my button down shirt in soccer mom blue finds its way unbuttoned and slid off, slung over the arm of the comfort cushioned sofa. As I slide my flats and jeans away, I continue to stare at this 27 year old beauty, to see if there is a hint of insolence in her eyes.

In my plain, white bra and underwear, I walk over to her as the fatter breasted, heavier hipped version of herself, standing still, in full dominance over her as she looks up at me. I mute the television, and its showing of the blonde mother in peril, telling my daughter to lie down on her back. I climb this underwear clad, well fed, figure eight form of mine on top of her, unable to restrain myself from the purity of another deep and fervent kiss, laid heavily on top of her in the fall of night.

The glow from the TV prophecy bathes us in the blue of ambient light, as I begin to press my groin to hers, coaxing her legs open, grinding these big, jiggly hips of mine to the Waltz of the Tribades, to a grinding rhythm of the prairie dolls in grieving. I am unable to hold this kiss, as I move my head to the side of her, beginning to slam myself down onto her repeatedly, feeling every ounce of pleasure the underwear cushions may provide.

What of her pleasure? What is her pleasure to me? There is only the pain of life *I* feel, and what *I* must do to drive it away. I hold nothing of this pounding rhythm back from her, feeling the warmth of her groin swollen beneath the cloth, and the pillows of flesh bound up in the soft sports bra fabric. The connections are made in my body, where inside is the burning heat of perversion, causing me to have to drive the message home to my daughter, that there will be no defiance of me, no insolence or disrespect, nor even the echo of disobedience. Every pound and squeeze, pound and squeeze, pound and squeeze of my buttocks brings my body closer to a place of *oh no*, a place that calls me as a drug, the place I would have rather died than to not have been.

The rhythm of the prairie dolls takes over the pound and squeeze of my hips, until the rest of my body feels as though it may come apart, and come back together in a feeling I cannot endure. Upon the driving of this pounding rhythm, the tension in my body breaks, and I hear myself bellow in her ear like the prairie she-cow that I am, grunting while the shaking takes its part of my flesh, in punishment for what I have done. I hold on to her while this bereaving passes, until the shaking in my body subsides.

I turn my head from the sofa cushion to the TV prophecy that plays, in time to see the remains of divine retribution, drift down beneath the waters of revenge, the ghostly, resurrected form of a dead woman, transformed into the beauty of an angel of vengeance from the shores of Heaven.

*Jonathan Lovejoy*

# A Mother's Secret

# 28

*I* HAVE USED DEPRAVITY to control her over the years. To dominate her. To make her emotionally dependant. To slowly, surely, systematically subjugate her will to mine. How much am I really to blame, for the person that she has become? An anthropophobic recluse, given to pessimism and dark premonitions about the future? What is it that I have done to my daughter, to make someone with such a profound gift become more of threat to mankind than any other human being ever born?

If I had been worth anything, she would be a PhD somewhere, pioneering research on telekinesis, unlocking the secrets of the human brain. Or perhaps she would be a secret military weapon, called upon to drop enemy aircraft into the land and sea. Oh, what a glorious and easy advantage she would give, in the air battles over land and sea! But when she was sixteen, when she told me she was never going back to school again, what did I do?

I gave her an enema.

In the heart of this twisted memory, my daughter has already suffered the indignities of something akin to an anal raping by me. I am but one of many mothers who share this painful secret, who have done this thing to their daughter in one form or another. And not many days past her anal raping, I felt depravity's call rise again inside me, causing me to want to make her suffer anally again, but this time in perverted variation, something born from my own mother's private obsession, which was done to me throughout my teenage years in secret.

I remember that Caroline Bourbon, my mother, would have died before she would have admitted to such a thing. But it was something that she had to do to me. And as though called up from the graveyard of my subconscious, this ghost took hold of me from my breasts to my groin (where I felt like I needed to piss myself from the arousal), and made me understand that as surely as the sun will set over the Kansas prairie, my daughter's bowels would be filled with water.

In the heart of memory, she has already spent a day away from solid food, learning what it feels like when a laxative takes hold. And the day after that, the time has come, when she is standing in broad hipped nudity in the bathtub, with me standing on the floor, with the classic white enema bag hung up on the shower curtain rod. I relish, I cherish this moment, as the enema nozzle pushes smoothly into her bottom, causing her to tense up and breathe on the edge of pain and suffering. I push the thin, white plastic tube deep up inside her. Until every inch times six is hidden away.

*Now squeeze*, I say. *I'm going to push the water in now.*

I watch her comply pitifully, her hands pushed hard against the shower walls, as I release the water down through the tube and into her backside, squeezing the bag to push the water in, so delighted when she yelps a little and tenses up all the more. What is it in me that lowers my head to her breasts, and makes me suck both of her nipples as though they tasted like strawberry glaze in July? It is a hunger that I feed, remembering how it felt to my own body when it was done to me, by a woman that no one would believe was capable of such a thing.

*Keep your butt squeezed, but relax. You're too tense…*

And when she relaxes, I notice that the white nozzle threatens to slide out prematurely. I so gladly push it back to its place deep inside her, bending her over, holding it while the water fills her insides, which I can feel pushing against her gut down below.

*Ow, it hurts*, she says so pitifully. But I can only stare down at the nozzle deep inside her rectum, glimpsing the rest of her body and her big, hanging breasts, drawing pleasure from what pain she feels in her bowels. Observing the nature of pain and suffering.

*Hold it in,* I say, but keeping my hand at the nozzle, knowing that she is trying hard to push it out. But to no avail. *Squeeze your buttocks*, I say, smacking her hard on the backside with my other hand, watching her push against the shower walls with her head down, moving the rest of her body around like one does when watering nature calls.

*I said hold it in,* I say sharply. *Hold still, its almost over. Just relax. Feel the water inside you. When it comes out you'll feel better than you've ever felt in your life. I promise. Now, hold still...*

The enema bag is nearly empty, and her poor abdomen is as tight as a drum. *Almost there, baby,* are the words that slip out of me, as I now begin to caress her big bottom with one hand, holding the nozzle in with the other. Such a valiant effort she is determined to give her mother, as she lowers her head and yells in loud frustration, which seems to activate the theater of my mind, when I held the nozzle into my mother's gigantic ass, while she was on her knees in the bathtub growling out loud like a she animal. In my mind, the nozzle that was in my mother slips through my hands and away, and the water sprays from her backside like a faucet on high, the spirit of which slides my hand away from the nozzle in my daughter, allowing it to shoot free, amidst a loud and gruff yell from her, with a blast of water from inside her bottom down to the bathtub below.

*You did so good,* I say to her, placing my finger gently into her bottom where the enema nozzle has come and gone. Holding my other hand at her breast. Kissing her gently on the mouth.

Gently.

*I* PUNISH MY DAUGHTER by fucking her.

Whether or not she is aware of it when it happens is immaterial. I look for any echo of negativity in the air. The slightest rise in tension is my opportunity to apply this perversion—to draw from her the awkwardness and discomfort I need, to satisfy the seed of lust planted and grown, where there is an endless meadow of perversion blossomed. From this meadow of depravity I am burdened to choose to make her suffer an enema again. But this, in the knowledge of years, where she knows that my satisfaction is to see her hold it in forever. To hold it in until I have taken my part of her suffering in full.

I have her on all fours in our big bathtub, with her already filled to suffering capacity. On her hands and knees, long breasted and obedient, her beautiful head of hair pinned all the way up, to better prepare for the business at hand—her beautiful face fully exposed. I am strapped on already, so she knows what is coming, even while I tape the special nozzle in place, so that with her normal strength, she could not push it out if she tried.

I step into the bathtub behind her, realistic member hanging down as a weapon, prepared to cut the life from her hopes of being free from me. *You will never be free of me,* is the echo inside my head, spoken by the sliding of the 10 inch monster into her from behind, into the proper place, while the enema nozzle holds the water trapped inside her bowels to perpetuity. She is doubly penetrated now, being fucked by her mother, being made to understand forever that to be born is to be cursed, and to live is to suffer.

"Hold it in," I say, in soft, high pitched tolerance, watching her nod her pretty head, while every inch times 10 is slid slowly up into her from the back, to cause further discomfort because of the sheer size of it, filling her up in the bowels and the womb with a mother's secret, with this craving for latter day satisfaction. Every cell in my body is pitched and programmed for this quiet, private moment, lost beneath the surface of history, beyond where seeing eyes could pry, or hearing ears could hear. The knowledge of this is power, the knowledge of the forbidden, drawing my hips back and forth in the style of the dog, the female rear entry, where the member probes deep inside her without mercy.

A sudden, steady four/four time begins between us, where we both understand that this rhythm cannot cease, until critical mass has been achieved, and both our bodies have suffered the loss of stability and control. The sound of my body slapping against hers only adds to what has already gripped my heart in fear, already pricked it in the cold waiting, the waiting for what is known and unknown, the feeling that will flash through me like a bolt of lightning in a thunderstorm.

"Yes. Hold it in," still a prisoner of the pounding, as insane as one who sits in an abandoned house with a drug pipe lit, or with a needle pushing death into their veins. "Oh, Jesus," I say, but with not the slightest hint of vulgarity, but with a profound sense of bewilderment, a cry for help from the heavenly hosts to take hold of me this time, and help me endure this trauma without passing out.

And my daughter is suddenly gripped in full, losing control of herself all at once, crying out in two high pitched shrieks of fear and agony, as the steady pounding continues of its own volition, bringing the name of God this time, as the lightning strikes me from in my bowels and groin, shooting pleasure into me that climbs the ladder of intensity, until it crosses over into pain, causing me to cry an angry warrior's yell into the small space around us, doubling over onto my daughter's back, barely able to breathe through the rapid beating of my heart, and the loss of my ability to think and reason.

# A Mother's Prayer

# 30

THE CELESTIAL BEAUTY of the Kansas night haunts me in my dreams, until I am aware only of being lifted from the earthly plane, drifting toward the stars in the Second Heaven. It overwhelms me with a sudden terror, causing me to jerk myself awake suddenly. It was as if my journey to the stars was impending and inevitable, more like a vision than a dream, making it seem as though I have only phased from one consciousness  to another. In this reality I lie awake in the bed, wondering where Venicia is, and how it is that it just felt like this entire house was in outer space.

I have to sit up in bed for just a moment, until the walls and the ceiling have full substance again around me. Even though its 2:30 in the morning, my young lady is nowhere in sight. One of the types of fear descends upon me in spirit, to cause cold twinges in my heart and the pit of my stomach, this being the Fear of Abandonment, trying to make me run around the house like a crazy woman in the nude, looking for wherever it is she has gone. But I'm rational enough to take a deep breath and calm my nerves, sliding my silken robe around my naked skin. Somehow, I already know she is not in the house, and I anxiously hurry down the stairs, past the big TV and out the back patio door.

The view of the Kansas night sky is pristine, with what seems like every star in the heavens clearly visible. I can't remember the last time I have seen a more brilliant starry sky, where my view is unencumbered by manmade light of any kind, as every light in the house is off, and the truth of mankind's insignificance is laid out in pristine clarity. High above the nighttime field, I see the stars that form a gigantic Northern Cross in the sky, perhaps more aptly named for the long necked, white water bird whose elegant beauty it represents. I know that somewhere in this blackness, my own Earth Swan is hiding from me, and looking up at these same stars, perhaps feeling her place among them like no other human being who has ever lived.

Suddenly, it seems like one of the many stars comes to life in the skies directly above me, sparking a great distance towards our southern view. The tiny earth comet streaks a bright warning across half the skyline, dying somewhere to the far left, over our field, toward the southern horizon.

It is perhaps the most unique disobedience in human history. I go back inside the house briefly, retrieving the little Maglite, going back outside with the light blaring, shaking it in the air over the wheat field, hoping that she'll answer me. But being that it is so late at night, did she remember to take hers with her? Is she really there?

As if to answer a mothers' prayer, I see a sheepish, guilty little light click on afar off, a great walking distance from the lawn into the field. Leaving my light burning, I begin my journey through the nighttime wheat field, wanting in part to catch a rare glimpse of our world from in the middle of the prairie field, and also to scare the panties off that disobedient little witch I gave birth to.

Before too many ticks of the night clock, I am finally able to see her directly, her white T-shirt contrasting well with the dark infinity around us.

"I couldn't sleep," she says. "I'll come back to bed in a little bit."

"Its alright. You don't have to rush. Truth is, I can see why you're out here. Especially when you get a chance to see shooting stars like the one I just saw. It went from the top of the sky… all the way over there."

I point toward the stars in the southern sky, watching her look wide eyed, lips tucked in quiet awe and humility.

"I thought I made it clear that you were not to do this again."

In the dark, I can see the pain of dejection on her face. It touches the sadistic side of myself. I step close to her, so that her white t-shirt is pressed to my silken blue robe in cushioned comfort.

"What am I going to have to do to make you stop? Keep you locked up in the basement? Whip you every day for a month? Start sending you to bed without all those delicious, fattening suppers you like to cook? How about those Barbie Dolls I keep letting you waste our money on? Without me, where are you going to live? What are you going to do?

What do you think the world would do it found out that somebody like you existed? They would *crucify* you. Worship you for a while. Then destroy you. All we have left... is each other. And our quiet little life out here in the middle of this wheat field. And I don't want you causing any more trouble in the sky. Look at me."

The look on her face, the devastation in her soul is an aura of hopeless misery. She lowers her head again, sniffing loudly in the dark.

"You may as well save the tears, honey. The more you cry, the worse its going to get."

She wipes both her eyes, sniffing again, still unable to look at me.

"How about I give you something that you'll remember this time? Hmm?"

"I won't do it again. I promise."

"It's too late for that, Venicia. You are a threat. A menace. You have to be made to understand that this power of yours is wrong. Its evil. And I don't want you using it any more."

She sobs once aloud, still unable to push her way through her nightmarish disillusionment to look at me.

"Go to your Barbie Doll bedroom and wait for me."

The beautiful young woman turns away in epic sorrow, walking quickly, nearly stumbling in the effort, her mouth half open in disbelief for what must be.

I watch her silhouette begin to darken, until I perceive her as a shadow in three dimensions, moving rapidly through the nighttime field toward the house. I look back toward the heavens, in full understanding that this is what I must do, and that in this very hour, I have to remind her that I am to be obeyed at all costs, and that she is about to become acquainted with the full meaning of pain and suffering.

# 31

*I*N THE UPPER ROOM, the glow of the lamp lights our little drama for the prairie dolls, so that they may see the beautiful girl's breasts bared for punishment. The two of us stand in our underwear bottoms, her with her hands clasped behind her back. Obedient. Compliant. Her face twisted with sorrow.

From the dresser, I lift the fiberglass cane, the black stick of death, that strikes fire in the body from the point of origin, as it endeavors to cut white skin to blood.

In the wake of my desire, I touch the cane to the front of her breast in warning, which causes her to flinch, followed by the sound of a booming explosion outside, which literally rocks the house to its foundation, making more than one of the prairie doll chorus lean forward tragically in their collector boxes and fall noisily to the floor.

The explosion that I hear cascades away from us, allowing the house to cease the violent shaking, as it fades further and further into the distance like roaring thunder. Though she stands still, her eyes closed, her hands behind her back, she can do nothing to hide the truth of what just happened.

The black stick of death is suddenly too heavy for me to hold. I return it slowly, carefully back to its place on the dresser, staring at the beautiful, topless woman in a renewed fascination, understanding that every cocoon must eventually break, and what emerges can bear no resemblance to what pitiful, pretty little thing it was before.

# 32

*I* BEAR no proximity to anything vaguely related to sleep, staying awake for the rest of the night, understanding two things. One, the tiger is off the chain. And two, she is hungry.

What control I thought I had over my daughter has gone the way of a wayward snowflake in the sun. It was here. It was pretty while it lasted. But now it is gone.

Any perverted suffering I cause her from here on, I'm sure, will be with her permission only. I had left her to her confusion, telling her to go to bed and go to sleep, hurrying down the late night stairs and out onto the prairie lawn, expecting to see a plume of fire and smoke in the distance. But when I got there, all I saw was the same blackness that I had just come from, and the same brilliant view of the summer sky. I had stood there stunned, my robe tied tight over my perverted bosoms, bound up in temporary retreat from their new reality.

How costly of a lesson could it have been? The energy she sent into the ground from where we were—what if she had turned that negativity toward me? A broken back, maybe. With her on the phone screaming to 911, wishing that she could have taken it back. The fear and confusion I felt at that moment may have been what I deserved, considering the way that I have used her to satisfy my own sickness, my own private sadism and depravity. But knowing her like I do, I know that she will spend her days focusing with all her might on other things, possibly even the foolishness of online education or job seeking, anything to try and have a normal life, to try and escape the horror of being kept from her calling.

What does it mean to see a white jackass in a dream? I don't need Joseph to interpret what I just saw, while sitting here on the living room sofa, as sleep threatens to finally overtake me. I relax and try to go back to sleep, unafraid to see myself on four legs again with long ears, but seeing instead a crashed car on an isolated Kansas highway. Then suddenly, a beautiful figure in red and star spangled blue flies out of the wreckage and lands on her feet, her fists on her hips in a stance of triumph.

Awakening with a start, I know that somehow, for whatever dark, dangerous reason, I have to give her permission to be who she is, and to be here for her as still her refuge, her place to go when her little world just doesn't make sense any more. And how can it ever, being able to do the impossible things she can do? The days of me suppressing those latent abilities just ended, and I can't help but wonder what in the name of God is looming over our next horizon.

My Amazon Princess is suddenly shuffling around upstairs. Pulled, no doubt, from the midst of an unrestful sleep. She begins walking down the stairs, sleepy eyed, hair a mess, looking at me in a worried, determined stare, bouncing the last two steps down to the floor. She strolls directly over to where I sit, leaning down to kiss me firmly on the lips.

"Are you okay," she says, sitting down beside me.

"Maybe I should ask *you* that."

"I don't know what happened. When you were gonna hit me, I just got so scared that—"

She suddenly tucks her lips and looks down. As if it is too fearful to remember.

What, honey? What happened?"

"I felt something inside me pushing out toward you. I stopped it and made it go into the ground. *It* wanted to grab you and twist you like bread dough, Mom."

"So, you were going to *kill* me."

"No, *I* wasn't. *It* was. I would never hurt you Mom, I swear to God."

"I know honey. And… I'm sorry I tried to hurt you."

"You were just being a parent. Trying to protect me from this."

Why am I unable to humble myself? To admit that between the two of us, I am the one to blame. Oh, God, how many painful punishments, how many rapings, paddlings and spankings have I given her, none of which she has deserved? Why can I not admit even to myself, that I was on the verge of graduating my sadism into full breast torture upon my daughter?

"No matter how much I try *not* to use it, Mom, that's never going to happen. It would be like asking a tree not to grow. It's happening on its own. And I have to turn it to the sky, or else."

"Did it just show up all of a sudden? Or have you felt it all this time? All these years?"

"I've been pulling down meteors for almost seven years. Even though I can't really see them, it's like I still know they're there."

"That big one a few months ago, that caught everybody's attention, the one recorded over that highway near here. Remember? Did you have anything to do with that?"

No answer.

"They said if it hadn't exploded in the air…"

In her silence is a plea for my discretion. A cry for mercy.

"I wanted to start pulling down satellites, space stations," she says. "But something inside wouldn't let me."

"How did you keep this from me?"

"I only needed to pull one down every now and then. I knew they'd just be shooting stars to you. But the other night, I started…*collecting* them. I didn't think you would be outside. You never come out at twilight for more than a few seconds every now and then. I just felt the need to collect as many of them as I could, and then bring them all down at once, to see what it looked like. It's something I have to do, Mom. No matter what you do to me I'm gonna have to do it."

That part of it, I *do* understand. When something terrifying is so much a part of who you are, that you know you would almost rather die than not let it happen. No matter whom it may concern.

"Be careful, honey. Please… be careful."

*Jonathan Lovejoy*

# The Skies Over Topeka, Kansas

*And the stars of heaven shall fall, and the powers that are in heaven shall be shaken.*

Mark 13:25

THE SKIES OVER TOPEKA, KANSAS are often on fire with falling stars, as the world turns toward the evening day.

It is her favorite time of the day or night to exercise her gift, which is to manipulate objects at great distances, causing them to move at her will. I rarely see her arms milling about, though sometimes her hair is aflight, in whatever mysterious breezes there are that appear around her. One of the times when I saw her arms move was during the bright light of late afternoon, when I heard a noise that was disturbingly familiar. When I had run outside to see the tragedy of her original calling return in fire and smoke, I saw her with both her arms extended, in deep concentration, while a passenger plane as big as a nightmare was cruising towards the open field not much higher than the top of a grove of tall trees. The great plane glided noisily past the girl in the wheat field, with a sound like screaming thunder, then I saw it rise rapidly again as if in full take off, with her staring after it in the same raised arm concentration. I can imagine that the Fear of Death was lifted from inside that airplane when it was ascending, as I'm sure that memories of the Thirty Nine Flights of Topeka had claimed their minds. The pilots will tell of how everything in the plane kept working fine, accept that they had no control over it whatsoever, as if the airplane were being controlled by an outside force that didn't let them go until Topeka was long gone. If there are any giggles to be had for her in this strange calling, I know it was at the thought of how she made them scream over the big open field out back.

What would she do to air travel around the world, if she decided  that 10 times a day, she would make the world understand that there is nowhere to hide, on the eve of eschatology? Nature has a way of placing all things in perfect balance. There is a reason that she is not comfortable around people, or anywhere in the natural flow of society. Eventually, there would be only death and destruction everywhere she went, and no one would be the wiser as to why. There would be no guns trained upon her, for why point a gun at a beautiful, innocent looking woman standing by, while the second floor of the mall is caving in and killing 200 people in the process? Who would know to handcuff and arrest the doll that was standing at the Empire State Building, when the glass and the concrete began to crash and shatter? Nature has seen to it that she is as disposed to lonerism as a mountain grizzly, tucked away safe and out of the way of the naïve fools that would get in her way. And sometimes, I think about that jackass that was me, trying to plug a geyser with a motorcycle wheel and a prayer.

The greatest meteor shower in human history lights up the skies after sunset, in the fading light of deep twilight. It is the classic dream of the so-called "meteor shower," which has rarely (if ever) shown itself to be so in any other event, which sees a spark of light per minute as a fiery deluge of some kind. On this July 4$^{th}$ twilight, high over the field nearby our home in isolation, there are streaks of white light sparking everywhere at once, with the occasional long, bright glow of blue or green, which holds the attention like nothing manmade can achieve. I notice that this huge, green fireball streaks all the way across the sky until it threatens to hit somewhere beyond the distant southern horizon, breaking apart into several smaller pieces before disappearing all together. And this, while the rest of the sky is already lit up with fiery streaks of silver light, giving credence to the image "falling star." This remarkable explosion of light lasts for well over five minutes, the finale to a half hour of celestial dust and debris being slowly drawn in over where we live.

After this last comet fire streak has come and gone, I watch the field of shooting stars go from thousands to hundreds, slowing down to scores and then dozens of little trails of light. These dozens taper off over the next few minutes, until the Marianna Meteor Shower again resembles the norm, which is a single wink of light every minute or so. I know that nowhere in the world this fourth of July, were the onlookers treated to anything quite like what I just saw. I am suddenly humbled to nothing by this girl's presence, as I wait for her to walk out of the wheat field to the back lawn. When she is barely out of the field and into the back yard, I hurry over to the woman that I love, the daughter I love, hugging her tight and sobbing like what she has never imagined that she would see, begging her to forgive me for the years of cruelty and for the part that I have played in the cause of her pain and suffering.

"*The skies were lit up this 4ᵗʰ of July with what astronomers are calling the greatest meteor shower in human history. It appeared as though thousands of shooting stars streaked across the sky in the space of 5 to 10 minutes, leading scientists to believe that the earth passed through a previously undetected cloud of space dust and debris, possibly left over from the trail of a comet or obliterated asteroid. This impromptu cosmic fireworks display concluded with the appearance of a very large, bright green meteor the size of a house, they say, that eventually exploded into smaller fragments over Topeka, Kansas before it completely vanished. One suburban woman who witnessed the Topeka Fireball was rushed to the hospital after she appeared to have fainted, but never regained consciousness. The cause of her death is yet unknown. I'm Cora Leeds, the Associated Press.*"

*Jonathan Lovejoy*

# Earth Goddess

# 35

M UNNATURAL AFFECTION for my daughter remains paramount. Even outside earlier this evening, as I crumbled under the weight of humility in her arms, my body was on fire with the need to be with her, to draw comfort from her in my own special way.

So much over the years, all the way back to when she was a child, we have been nursemaids, the two of us, even milkmaids for a time, when the thirteen year old girl she was would be standing with me in the nude, holding up one of my big, round milk bottles with both hands, pulling on it with her mouth until she drank her fill. I would stand there with my hands on my hips or behind my back, sometimes caressing her beautiful little face, never being able to resist a visible tremble in my body. And it may be end of the world remarkable, that she had the mindset to stop sucking and look directly up at her mother and say *"did you cum?"* which would both embarrass and annoy me at the same time, to which I would just smile a little and tell her to keep sucking. And this, she would do, sometimes picking up the other one to start anew, which would send new bolts of lightning straight to my groin. Sometimes, every sucking pull on the other breast would raise the feeling higher and higher while she nursed, until my body reacted on its own, and Venicia would be a witness to her mother's orgasm, watching me start to shake from the hips up, until I had to double over from the tension breaking in my body. I learned early on that I am an Orgasm Queen, an Earthquaker, a woman prone to very strong and multiple orgasms. But oddly enough, this was not the case when I was with my husband before he died. This ability came upon me when my daughter and me began this little latter day secret of ours. The touch of her lips anywhere on my body is a threat to its stability, as is the reverse, when I am kissing, licking or sucking any part of her. I am perhaps uniquely prone to an 'earthquake' from just sucking her breasts alone. It truly is the Nun's Intercourse for me, as it is often the only stimulation I need to get off.

There is a line in a recent, brilliant movie about a rogue planet crashing into the Earth, where one of the sisters makes a suggestion that they should meet on the terrace and enjoy a drink at the world's devastation. The depressed sister, the *Melancholia* sister responds that she thinks her idea is stupid. Then she says with bitter sarcasm, *"Why don't we just meet on the fucking toilet?"*

And I say to that, why the Hell *don't* we meet on the fucking toilet? I always seem to have some of my strongest orgasms on the toilet with Venicia, sometimes as she sits on the throne itself, while I sit heavily on top of one of her legs astraddle, with one of her great, long breasts pulled

daughter perversion, a secret spread from the slums to the suburbs, across the length and breadth of this nation and around the world.

I take my part of this latter day secret, pulling at my daughter's breast like a starving child, squeezing the other one, holding onto it without letting go. She looks down at my pathetic condition, noticing the anguish in my face as I suck so hard and continuously, as though frustrated that her breasts can give no milk. It is something we have never committed to trying, as mine have lactated almost continuously for fifteen years, being so easily reactivated if they run dry for a time. Even arousal itself will sometimes start them dripping, which will make her attack them hungrily to make them finish what they have started.

Her attention is at one of my nipples now, pinching the milk from it while I lay in her lap sucking hers. I can feel the milk dripping down the side of my breast as she squeezes, causing me to remember my mother on her hand and knees in the nude on the bed, accepting a brutal naked paddling from me as both her breasts drip slowly onto the bed. This image does strike a fire in my groin, and I begin a low pitched groan suddenly at my daughter's breasts, which turns into deep, muffled grunting as the tension breaks in my body, while I hold on to my daughter's breasts for support, as the wave of latter day thunder and lightning passes through.

# 36

*M*Y MOTHER was a breast queen. Not because of any great size of them, they played their tragic melody in an E minor key. Not because of any particular cosmetic perfection or beauty; they hung very long against her body, with great, dark areolas irregular in their calling, with large nipples that grew to alarming size when aroused. And those were perhaps the source of what she was under her clothes and behind closed doors. Caroline Bourbon was a breast queen because she was erotically obsessed with her own breasts, and the breasts of other women (making her a *breast goddess,* perhaps). But these 'other women' were only the breasts of mine, the breasts of her daughter from the age of thirteen.

My body shook before the end of the third pass of her lips across my young nipples, assuring her that she had found her calling in life. And she was rewarded by the blossoming of my body over the next three years; I was balloon breasted and bubble bottomed by my sixteenth birthday. And she had found a partner in this crime of perversion, all done without my father's knowledge, mostly when he was at work, but sometimes when he was in the house; with us locked in the bathroom where she had snuck in when I was using it or taking a bath, or sometimes in the middle of the night when he was asleep. Our weekend mother daughter outings were numerous and without fail, sometimes driving to the most isolated place we could find out of town and parking like horny teenagers, which I was, which she took full advantage of throughout my teenage years and into my adulthood, ending only after I met and married my husband.

*"Please, in the name of God don't do it,"* she had said to me in tears, breaking down the walls of pretense, letting me understand that I was all that she had left that she gave a damn about—her Bible, her church, her dead husband's memory, none of it mattered to a *"a copper cent"* she had said. *"After what you and I have with each other, how can you possibly get married,"* she had said, the pain inside so profound, that the tears fell even though her expression was hardly anguished at all. And the truth is, though I had insisted to her that I loved him, the truth was that I *liked* him and *tolerated* him just enough, using him to get away from my mother's control. I loved him, to be sure, but there were times when I laid in the bed in tears, imagining that I would have to spend the rest of my life at his sexual beckon call.

By the age of 21, by my junior year in college, I was ready to stop with my mother, ready to move on with my life—even though a part of me still needed the secret life of a motheress, a woman who secretly performs sexual favors on her mother in private. A visit home from campus was the highlight of her days and years, because she knew that the two of us were going to sin like Adam and Eve.

In the heart of memory, the rains of my fervent discontent do fall, over the place where my mother is buried. Why is it that I have to be burdened by fear and guilt at her grave, because she lies here of her own doing? A pain so deep and profound that she expressed it through a hanging, using a six foot step ladder to climb naked to a branch in our back yard tree. Kicking that ladder over when she was ready, to let a two foot rope take care of the business at hand.

My mother's best church friend had to suffer the devastating Fear of Discovery in the fading light of day, somewhere between sundown and the evening day, when she saw the naked figure of the widow hanging by the neck from the tree, with the ladder laid on the ground underneath her. Why should I shed tears at her burial, refusing even to be there with my husband? I had to be there alone with the wind and the rain, to read this ironic name alone—a woman who played Super Christian in public all my life, with a last name like the sinful drink, and a secret so abominable that the mere thought of such a thing might put someone in danger of Hell fire if they're not careful. As to what God thought of us in those hours of iniquity, she never mentioned, as her shadow self was truly a different personality inside and out. Oddly enough, when I wasn't being punished, the person she was then was probably the best friend I ever had, more friendly and likeable, more willing to talk about the bullshit which is public life, even telling me of the hypocritical things she herself was aware of. But even so, she was unafraid to turn on a dime, to suddenly stop being nice for no good reason, simply because she didn't like my tone of voice, or if she didn't like the way I responded to her passion, or if an unpleasant thought from the day were to cross her mind. She kept me on an emotional roller coaster, she made me walk the high wire with no net, being unafraid to even slap me, with no other explanation than *"because you're full of sass, that's why."* But during my college years, I became less afraid of the southern pole of her personality, guarding myself in preparation for it, until she understood that there was no need to try so hard anymore to catch me off guard with a sharp sick in the side. By the time I was 21, I was a full blown Mother Lover, and I performed my calling with every part of who I was—spirit, soul, mind and body.

In the heart of this tragic memory, in days just before the ladder under the tree, I am a twenty one year old woman of means, home to visit my church going mother, who hides her beauty in no makeup, and her sensuality in plain, country attire. In the heart of our darkest dream, we stand close together fully clothed, staring each other in the eyes without hypocrisy, and without remorse. *"Are you going to do it me?"* she asks. *"Are you going to punish me?"* My response is a deep and powerful pressing of my lips to hers, while our tongues meet unseen, and the grunting of her voice is deep and filled with passion. I begin to undress her, but with a slow burn, and not an explosion of pointless ripping and tearing and tossing of fabric. My lips are at her neck as the zipper of her dress comes down, un-kissing her just long enough to slide her southern flower made dress off her shoulders, down to her waist and to the floor down below. She stands there in her slip, cleavage bubbled up in her tight bra, watching her daughter take her plain navy dress off, button by button, then sliding it down and away, to reveal the white bra fabric and matching tiny underwear, barely able to cover the spread of my hips, and the vastness of my heavy bosom. Two inch navy pumps still in place, I step back over to her, to cause the collision of worlds, the mashing together of our breasts still in cleavage cloth, causing the beautiful, older woman to look down at our skin pressed together, rising above our bras in warning of the approaching tide, of the impending wave of devastation which is to come. I return my kiss to her, in greater fullness of intent, kissing her long and hard while she is in her slip. Letting my hands slide down the length of the silken fabric, gripping both her big, soft buttocks in a full squeezing, making her writhe just enough, grabbing the back of my head in the mother-grunting, the deep, sensual sounds of arousal from deep within. I squeeze her buttocks again over the slip, causing her to release the kiss and hold her head back with her eyes closed. Instinct grabs my hand and powers it to a heavy slapping of one of her buttocks, then one more with a squeeze, until I see the suffering in her face appear. I slide the slip down from her shoulders, past her breasts and the magnificent curve of her waist, exposing the impossible, a set of hips spread out to infinity from the smallish waist, to create from the front alone the burning of desire in all humanity. I take the slip down past her black flat shoes, sliding it to the side, then taking each shoe off her stocking feet. I run both hands up one leg to the top of the stocking, feeling her leg twitch in betrayal, as I pull the stocking down slowly past the knee, then down to the ivory skin of her foot, pulling it with authority past her toes and away. I do this same climb to the top of her other leg, grabbing the stocking and sliding it down, past the toes of her other foot, kneeling down on both my knees for a moment, kissing the tops of both her feet, looking up to see her judge me as ridiculous or inferior, but seeing only her with her eyes closed, her mouth slightly open and head tilted far back in the calm of uneasy acceptance, and the arrival of the threshold of desire. I go back up to the top of this highest tree, this great sequoia of lust and desire, placing my tongue in ice cream lick to one side of her neck, and then the other, hearing the grunts inside transformed to bellowing, of which she is unashamed, to signal the arrival of her apocalyptic need.

*You need me to fuck you, don't you?*

*Yes,* she says.

*Then let me hear you say it.*

*Fuck me.*

I grab the back of her underwear with one hand, pulling it tight up into her massive bottom, evoking a deep breath from her.

*Say the words, 'I need you to fuck me.'*

*I need you to fuck me,* she says, staring at me nearly wide eyed, in serious determination and intent. I reach behind her and unlatch the big bra, letting the big, long breasts fall free and bulbous against her body. My own desire is suddenly at the same plateau, causing me to step back from her, reaching back and undoing the latch on my own boulder holder, sliding it free and clear of its purpose under the sun. My mother looks up and down the length of my body, her face intensely anguished, even shaking her head once, as if in disbelief that the desire of her heart is coalesced before her in shape and form. I step back over to her in utter confidence, navy heels and stockings still in place, pushing the nipple of my right breast to her right breast, where both of our left breasts are a universe away from one another. When the nipples touch, her entire body shudders, as though she was just hit with a chill too cold to endure. I take my breast by the hand, and rub the nipple firmly against hers, exhaling once with my own head back, relishing the feel of her oversized nipple to mine. I rub my nipple against hers in a fever, until she says *please stop...*

*please stop or you're gonna make me cum*. This, I do. Knowing that for her, it is far from idle talk. I kiss her on the lips again, then her neck, her shoulders, then a single kiss to both nipples (both twitching her body just once), then down to the curve of her waist, biting in, pulling a powerful sucking kiss as I slide the underwear down and away, to reveal the full glory of her smooth shaven nudity, and the beckoning of it to my lips and tongue. I lean forward, pressing a kiss to it, being reminded of her body's sensitivity as one of her legs spasms in warning that she is ready for what must be. I take my shoes off at last, then sliding out of my stockings and underwear, taking up the member that lies in wait for us on the bed. I pick up the tangle of straps, stepping into the harness and sliding it up to my hips. *Is that your cock,* Mother says. *Are you going to fuck me with it?* I turn her no answer, as I calmly tighten the leather straps, pulling them tight, so that I can feel the soft leather pushing against my groin. I fear that from the tightening of the straps alone, I may shudder. *Come here to me,* I say. The woman walks over to where I am, her face now burdened with something close to a frown. I turn her toward the bed, standing her up straight, able to see her reflection in the mirror across the room. Ignoring the dejected woman in the mirror, I focus my energy into a back pendulum swing of the hand, bringing it down and around to the skin of her big backside as hard as I can, making her draw a breath of pure shock. This, I do a second time in the same place, which causes her to lose her breathing altogether, losing it in a shudder of uncertainty. And then, I bring the palm of my hand to her backside a third and final time, which is enough to make her lower her head, and let out a loud straining grunt of pure agony. This burning of her skin is enough, and I pull her loosely pinned, dark blonde hair hard, pulling her back toward me, pushing my tongue deep into her mouth that she may give suck, and bless her body for the undertaking that must be. I tell her to lay on the bed and onto her back. I climb to the place between her legs, sliding forward on my knees, tapping the member to the front of her, which causes her to grab her own gigantic breasts and to grunt loudly just once, staring up at me in a look of frustrated anticipation.

*I'm going to fuck you, Mother.*

*I know.*

*And no matter how much you beg, I'm not going to stop.*

I push the head of the member into her, bringing forth such a pitiful calling of *Oh, God,* as if she knows that this is the beginning of the end of her, and that she is about to be made to die screaming. Every thick inch times eight I slide into her, until she is filled up to her womb, pulling both her nipples up once in brief sucking, then laying heavily down on top of her, staring in her eyes, telling her to push our breasts together. The feel of this causes me to hold my head back for just a moment, to gauge the feeling in the Triangle of Needs, the area from my breasts to my bowels and my groin. A single squeeze down lets me know already that this inside her is a part of my body, and that I will suffer the same devastation as she. My hips, I raise up high, and slam down low just once, watching the madness appear in her eyes, feeling the delayed, bellowing reaction in her voice, the gruff, roaring exclamation of future tragedy.

*I'm gonna have to fuck you.*

*I know,* she says. A whining, whimpering voice. *Promise me you'll have mercy.*

*I can't do that.*

*But you know when it feels too good I can't take it.*

*Just hold on to me.*

She wraps her arms tightly around me, holding her legs far back, whimpering as if on the edge of a weeping with every thrust, as I settle into a rapid and hard rhythm, which pushes out from her voice the edges of a weeping bordering on epic, to justify the appearance of tears that have already begun. The woman of straw is a weeping goddess beneath me, barely able to draw a full breath, as the waves flash a flood into every part of her body. As I find our perfect four/four time, the rhythm of one, two, three, four, her crying turns into pleading sobs, a sobbing that is genuine, to reflect the power of what she feels in her mind, and the release of months of pent up energy into her body. I raise my head up from beside hers, to look at the growing madness on her expression, stopping, taking her breath away with a deep kissing, then taking hold of both her arms and pinning them to her sides, beginning the pounding rhythm again, returning her to a greater state of weeping, where it is now a series of loud, womanly whimperings, as the sound of a woman being tortured beyond endurance. *Please, don't do it to me* are the breathless syllables I hear wept at me from somewhere in her crying voice, making me have to focus, to deliver a harder, stronger rhythm. And this, I do. Hearing her loud, whining and whimpering transform suddenly into loud, long screams, deep woman screams of fear and pain, with her head thrown back as far as it will go, as I hold her down immobile, slamming myself into her without pity. Her loud, forceful screaming grabs a hold of my hips, driving me up and down into her without the ability to stop, until I feel a sudden, pissing twinge appear, igniting an inferno of pleasure around it that explodes into my bowels and my groin, flooding without mercy up to where our breasts meet, to cause a sudden loss of control in my body, and I hear somewhere beyond her screams, the sound of a high pitched shriek for the ages, and a feeling that my mind and body are being burned to devastation and ruin.

# The Blood of

# Strawberries

# *37*

ORDS from the flow of time and history, as they burden the heart and mind. Yes, I am a motheress of the highest order, as is my daughter alike in kind. And I am here to testify that the timeline repeats itself, over and over again, and I am ill prepared for what my daughter is going to do to me at this moment. In my little country kitchen, my hands are busy with my strawberry delight (not Venicia), cutting *real* strawberries at the counter, to glaze them to death in this red mystery substance, that puts the pounds on me at the top and the bottom. Cool whip on the top of this and yellow cake at the bottom, to fill up my bra and underwear to bursting. Some would accuse me of being fat, unless I stand up in tight jeans and a t-shirt. Then they would just accuse me of being fat assed and fat breasted, which is an unfortunate truth I cannot escape. Damn my mother.

The jeans I wear suddenly burn with a violent slap to the back of them. I turn and look at the beautiful brunette in her ponytail braid, knowing that her mischievous stare is laced with malevolence. She stands close behind me—pressing the front of herself hard to my backside. Biting my ear. Whispering.

"They don't even do that anymore, remember?"

"We can start trying again tonight though," she says. "Can't we?"

"Is that what you want?"

"I'm gonna give you what *you* want, when you finish those strawberries."

She takes my hand, and begins to lick the fingers deeply in pure, comic carnality, which suits her like I know she cannot imagine. The sight of her with my thumb in her mouth titillates me down to the core of who I am.

"I'm gonna go upstairs," she says. Speaking the words softly onto my lips. "Then I want you to wash your hands… and come up to my room."

Without another word, she turns and walks from the kitchen to the living room staircase, bouncing in shapely form up the stairs and away, leaving me with my hands still red with the blood of strawberries.

What functioning addict of the grape can resist a glass of sweet red wine elixir? I notice that my hands are trembling as I dry them with a paper towel. A touch of bewilderment laced with shame flashes through as I leave the strawberry delight to itself, walking these Mom Hips to the stairs, bouncing up behind wherever it is that my beloved daughter could have gone.

I go into the upper room, where the prairie doll chorus lives over a hundred strong, decorating two of her walls from the floor to the ceiling. All staring in wait like spectators in their respective Opera House balconies, looking down on what generational tragedy must unfold. Then suddenly, from behind the closet door steps Sapphira, Goddess of the Strap On.

"You are in so much trouble," she says. Holding it while she walks toward me. The epic size of her breasts is only enhanced by the male member hanging down. How she manages to look so athletic and natural wearing that thing, with that face and those impossible curves is a mystery.

The types of fear are many, and uniquely distinguished.

"And who says I'm in the mood for this kind of trouble?" (My clit trying to push through my pants, that's who.) "I was trying to fix us some dessert."

"I've got your dessert," she says. Smiling. Swinging the big, *ten* inch thing round about. Like a propeller.

"I'll be back when I'm done, young lady. Maybe."

I turn to leave on the whims of motherhood, feeling a sudden and distinct block to my motion, like trying to push the north sides of two strong magnets together. The feeling whirls me around and holds me immobile, as she walks slowly over to me, with a more somber look of deeper malevolence, and profound knowledge of tragic inevitability.

Her fingers appear at the buttons of my pink collar shirt. Taking them down one by one, until my shirt is open. She slides it down and away from my arms, tossing it to a place that only the prairie doll chorus can tell.

"Take off your bra," she says, walking over to the closet again. "Leave your jeans on."

This, I do. Giving the big things some much needed air to breathe. I turn my head, dropping the bra to the floor nearby. When I look around again, she emerges from the closet with what has to be the biggest *wooden paddle* in God's Creation.

Among these is the Fear of Pain.

"Where did you *get* that?"

"That package that came yesterday. Remember?"

"My God, I thought it was a Barbie Doll," I say, my hand at my naked chest. My mouth is wide open.

"Turn around," she says. Full blown, motherline hypocrisy descends, making me tilt my head in false shock, as if I have no idea from whenceforth this fire burns.

"Okay, I'll do this... if it's what you need," I say, turning my back to her.

"Put your legs together. Hands in front. Stand still."

I do all of this, still burdened by the inability to accept responsibility for my part in who it is she has become. A strap on dick wearing, Momma's ass paddling beauty queen.

In private.

"Do you know what a P.A.W.G. is, Mom?"

"A what?"

When the big paddle slams into my pants, I let out a loud, deep scream, leaning forward, turning to look at her as if she is insane.

"Oh, my *God* that burns. How many times are you going to hit me with that thing?"

"Turn around, Mom. Hold still."

This, I do. With fear and regret coming at me like shadows in the twilight.

The second fire slams a loud *whack* into the room, to elicit another scream. But this time, the scream is laced with sorrow, and the echoes of an emotional breakdown.

"Please, honey. It *hurts,*" I say, the last syllable choked off in warning. She walks over to me, Sapphira, holding her instrument of Divine Torture.

"Shhh," she whispers in my ear. "You can take it."

"Alright. I will."

For the sake of whatever drives my daughter at this moment, I gird my loins, literally, preparing them in my mind for the burning of blue and black fire, for the taste of what fiery comeuppance is overdue. But when the third blow slams into my being, the agony of my lifetime wells up after the fiery scream, and I shake my head, beginning to sob like a little girl after the whipping of her life.

"Please... I can't. I cannot take another."

My sobs continue, with my face in both my hands, my squeaking voice in the cave of my palms, coloring my sobs with an echo of the hopelessness they betray.

I hear the paddling wood take its place on the dresser, giving me space to relax in this cry. My daughter comes over to me, and I turn and hug her around her neck, in full, deep squeaking sobs that touch her deep in her soul.

"I'm sorry... I'm sorry for all the times I hurt you..."

Any further words I hope to speak are pressed away. Mashed out of existence by the feel of her lips against mine—so unafraid to wet her own face with the tears of my crying, and to drink in the wine of what sorrow and regret I feel. I can feel my own lips trembling against my daughter's tongue, against what depraved comfort she offers me to partake, as she hugs me tight, and kisses both my soul and my body to oblivion. From the wet kiss she moves to my wet face, adding to it with the full palette of her tongue to my cheeks, giving mild and brief suck to every inch of my face, to my eyes and back down, until I feel as though I may crumble from the power of this strange pleasure I feel.

My daughter guides me over to her grand, elegant light oakwood bed, with its unique oval mirror in the center. She kneels down and slides my jeans down from my hips, slipping them past my bare feet, then quickly returning to my pink silken undies, sliding them so quickly down and away. Kissing the tingly, itchy flesh on my bottom, surveying the three huge paddle welts and the skin already at the edge of deep red and blue. She sits me on the edge of the bed, laying me down on my back, guiding my head toward the mirrored oak, to tuck me away in her country middle class luxury. She need but touch the front of both my nipples with her hand, to send shivers to my spine and downward, until I am on the edge of a visible shudder, as I stare at her in wonder of what mysteries she might have yet to reveal. On her knees, as she slides her fingers from my breasts to my stomach, I am at last unable to fight the trembling, and I can see my waist quivering at her very touch, and the fearful waiting for what is yet to come.

I dare not hope, nor dream this thing she threatens, as she replaces her touch with kisses at my naval, causing my body to convulse one mighty time, then tighten up as she kisses me at the bottom of my waist again, moving down to the top of my thigh. She opens my legs, to take gentle part of my inner thigh, making me hold my breath, as each kiss moves toward the center of myself, where the heart of this fervent desire lies in wait. And after a brief eternity, on the far end of the longest second in human history, what I feel next carries me aloft, to cause me to have to look to the ceiling, to try and find a place beyond it to focus, that I may not drift apart into invisible elements, and lose myself to what cannot be imagined, to a sensation that cannot be foretold. And then I feel a second flash of this warm sucking at this proper place, at this improper place, which threatens to make me call upon Heaven to have mercy, to give me strength to survive this knowledge of good and evil. And then, a third and mighty sucking pulls at this place again, to bring the first echoes of the weeping that I feel, the first part of the death that rests inside me. I breathe the best that I can, doing what I can to abstain from sobbing as I struggle through the fourth, the fifth, the sixth, and at last a seventh sucking pull from down below, which I hear ended upon the sound of a kissing pull away, and a merciful and unmerciful breath upon the place where my devastation lay. Her kisses return to my inner thighs, to disperse and expand what suffering that grows, carrying back to my waist in kissing, then up toward the mountains of soft flesh, giving one nipple a gentle suck, to create another visible shudder in my body. I know that it would take but a few nursing pulls at my nipple to send me into orbit, and to make me long for the mercy of death and the grave. But she spares me, for the moment, moving up to my face, to return the perfumed sweat of where she was, to force me to partake of this sweet, of this forbidden taste that I am driven to devour from her tongue. From this kiss, I drink depravity in all its glory, breathing, swallowing in victory, of what otherworldly anomaly this is, and what apocalyptic secrets there are that lay hidden from the Eyes of Blind. I open my eyes from the kiss removed, to see her anguished beauty raise up, and return to her purpose, to the task at hand, taking the large member into her hand, tapping it, rubbing it across the place where her lips and tongue just were—rubbing it firmly in warning of what is going to happen, of what is going to make me long for the comfort of the grave. And then, at the end of this age of womanhood, she slides the head of Sapphira's Arrow into me, to cause me to have to sob already, and to beg her with spoken words to please have mercy on her mother, and to remember how much I love her. But she will hear none of it, as she slides every inch times ten all the way up inside me, holding it still, watching me hold my head back with my eyes closed in grief and suffering. She guides my legs up and open wide, climbing back to my lips, that I may taste my daughter's suffering sweet, and feel her growing power over the life and death of me.

With my legs held back, grabbing hold of her, I hold on as she pushes a long, steady thrust, crying out once from the pain of so large a member pushed inside me. Moving my face roughly against hers, returning my lips to hers again, that I may feel her tongue fill my mouth, and take my breath away. When she thrusts again, I can hear the sound of my own voice, straining to be heard in the bellowing of an animal, so deeply muffled by her lips and her tongue clamped to mine. From this cue, she begins to slam the member into me without ceasing, that she might feel the vibrations of her mother's voice going deep into her body. She thrusts this pain into me without ceasing, releasing the kiss to take a breath, that we both may hear the power of a woman's pain, and the tragic force of her suffering unto death. Then suddenly, she ceases the pounding rhythm. Taking both my hands, guiding them down to the side of my body. In the next instant, I feel the gentle wrapping of these bands of bondage, which are her arms wrapped around me, holding me immobile underneath her. The weight I feel is suddenly incredible, enough so that I know that there can be no salvation, and no deliverance from suffering.

As she lays so hard and heavy down on top of me, I feel her stop moving, relaxing her body, yet the weight and power of her grip is incredible. Then suddenly, from the midst of this, I begin to feel life down below, a living thing deep inside me, as the member pushed in is rolled around the walls of me, as if it suddenly has the power to *move* on its own. The movement is enough to make me afraid, as I am on the edge of a full blown panic underneath her, until she whispers the word of our past comfort into my ear, *milk, milk, milk,* to remind me that she has not abandoned me to a malevolent spirit, and that this will be a death achieved through an end of the world pleasure forbidden. The movement of Sapphira's Sword deep up inside me cuts directly through my resistance, until the pain and discomfort have gone, and there is only left the fear of what impossible pleasures there must be. The movement of Sapphira's Sword inside me, the sliding of it round and round causes me to have to begin to call for mercy already, knowing that screams will be my only fortress against this terror. Lying still, pinned to immobility, my legs held back by what power this is, I hear my voice begin to echo from the past, the words *please don't do it, please don't do it to me,* as the moving of Sapphira's Fire extols an icy heat, to begin the climb to the mountain high, of which there is only fear, and the dread of the unknown. She holds me still and tight, neither of us moving a muscle, but with my face contorted by terror, and my voice sobbing in fear. And suddenly, I feel the icy fire ignite the rest of my body inside, whirled into an inferno by the turning of Sapphira's Member, which raises me up to a place too high and fearful, and I have to begin to wail, but as only a prelude to a scream. What sensation this is hath surely never been achieved, as the member moves about my insides with a steady and rhythmic mind of its own, to throw me over the edge of the world's highest cliff, where I begin to scream at the top of my lungs, unable to move a muscle, unable to protect myself from the waves of power flowing through every inch of my mind and body.

HE ARMAGEDDON ORGASM torments the theater of my mind. This tragic thing that my daughter wiggled up into me three nights ago, still haunts me through the day and night, until sometimes I have to stop whatever little task I am doing, and just sit and stare into space. As I walk the summer park trail, gazing at the condemned souls milling about, I can only think upon that woman who lives in my house with a mixture of renewed love and fear. I had worked for such a long time to rid myself of the anxiety I had towards the girl, which really started I think, when she was only five, when the first of the Thirty Nine Flights of Topeka came down.

What is an Armageddon Orgasm? It is one that makes a woman scream to the top of her lungs, I guess. Different from the Weeping Orgasm, or the Siren, both of which I have had many times over the years. But I guarantee that few women have ever experienced what I had to endure three nights ago, when an orgasm causes you to have to scream loud enough to wake the dead. It is probably the same principle of first contact that has been tormenting me since it happened, the unwritten, unspoken law of human interaction with superthrilling events—like skydiving, or riding a roller coaster for the first time. Both of these acts elicit cries of the damned—a scream of the ages from those who become their victims. This is the principle of first contact, that requires us to be terrified of a dramatic experience the first time.

Either Heaven on Earth or Hell on Earth, it doesn't matter. We can adapt to the trauma, until that fear becomes the selling point, the very thing that keeps us going back over and over again. This can even apply to the abused, especially, those who are free to leave their abuser under their own power. They continue to provoke an abusive response from whom they are with, sometimes without realizing it, because they have become hooked on the drama—hooked on playing the role of the victim, literally getting off on it. It is why some people who were never prone to violence, suddenly become violent criminals when they are with certain people—they don't realize until they are sitting behind bars that they have been cuckolded, tricked into turning into the Incredible Hulk or the Savage She-Hulk, by someone who has taken up the role of professional victim, who is content to live life as a bitchy assed drama queen.

These are the ones who give victims a bad name. Masquerading as those who were thrown out of a moving car at 60 mph, rather than those who opened the door and jumped. These are the ones who walk with the grizzly bear, who bless the bear with the hugs and kisses and petting they need—until the mood strikes, and the human pulls out a sharp pointed stick, and secretly jabs it into the grizzly bear's side. When this poor animal rages in the agony of pure instinct, when all Hell breaks loose, the secret antagonizer is satisfied two fold—they have enjoyed the end of the world thrill of survival, and they enjoy the end of the world thrill of universal compassion, being celebrated as a helpless victim of someone else's cruelty. These are the ones who cry wolf, who lie in their motivations and intensions—until disaster strikes, and either the hospital ward or the cemetery become their realities. Or for the antagonized grizzly bear, a jail cell or a coffin.

But then there are those such as myself, who have been lured into the psychology of abuse—which is who I was with Caroline Bourbon, who took every opportunity to make me understand that I was going to be belt whipped or sodomized because *she* wanted it, whether I deserved it or not, which no one ever deserves but they get it done to them anyway. These are victims of the unprovoked abusers, the Proactive Abusers, the ones who are sick and in need of professional help, who look for every chance they get to make another person suffer. This 'proactive abuse' is passed down from generation to generation, flowing through the motherline reserves, until one day, the mother looks at her daughter with unprovoked contempt, and understands that somehow, some way, she must find a way to punish her.

And when the mother cannot easily provoke the daughter to negativity, when the daughter gives her no reason to legitimately punish her, the seed of abuse planted by birth still grows, and the daughter becomes a true victim of her mother's perversion. Being hurt behind closed doors, whether or not in the name of discipline, but merely to satisfy her latent urge to cause her daughter pain and suffering. This is the seed of sadism. Which, when properly instituted, produces a victim who grows accustomed to it. This is the seed of masochism. When the unfortunate girl or young woman grows to a tragic need, a dark instinct, that causes them to crave their mother's punishment. This yin and yang singularity, this circular dependence happens so often without the woman's knowledge; Mom needs to bitch, Daughter needs to be bitched at. And they do it without realizing that it is happening.

But then there are those who are a victim of forces stronger than tendency, louder than an echo. These are they, when the mother slams her thirteen year old daughter up against the refrigerator for no good reason accept that she is in a bad mood and that the daughter 'looked at her the wrong way.' The feeling may pass between the two of them like a ghost or a spirit, spreading from their hearts upward and downward, until *every* part of their mind and body are affected. And somewhere in their souls, they feel the unspoken truths: *I nearly pissed myself when I mashed my daughter up against the refrigerator,* and *I almost peed myself when Mom mashed me up against the refrigerator.*

A warm breeze comes from somewhere off the morning Kansas prairie, from somewhere past the trees in the park, blowing some unknown message of warning to the people down below. I am lucky enough to have found an empty picnic table by the woods, where I sit in busty repose, staring at the grassy and woodsy landscape around me. My dark blue jeans are tight over my butt and thighs, and truthfully, if this peach button down shirt were any tighter, it would pop open on my next deep breath.

I feel like a stuffed sausage in these clothes. I wish I was back on the farm, with a t-shirt tucked into my favorite faded blue jeans, getting ready to have a piece of strawberry delight, in the arena where the prairie dolls live and breathe the ghostly limits of their calling.

# The Twelve

# Moons

# 39

THE FULL MOON rises big and crimson over the Kansas prairie, low above the wheat fields after sunset, in the fading light of the evening day. I have enjoyed the rare day away from the brick farmhouse, away from our mother daughter prison, now riding the country streets of this town, at the edge of another twilight over the plains. Whenever I leave the choking confines of the city and suburban streets, I am always glad that this is the life that was chosen for me, and that I no longer have to play the suburban game. *All of them witches,* are the words that echo in my spirit, the suburbs taken over around the world by Desperate Housewife Syndrome, wives dominating and controlling their husbands and children through every emotional whim—if Mom's not happy, *we're* not happy, spreading infidelity and divorce like a disease, until the landscape is populated by families torn apart, and the lives of children and husbands torn asunder. So many of us use our *cunts* as an excuse to cause end of the world trouble for everyone in our lives, then passing the blame for our destroyed families to everyone around us, when it was us who just plain got bored and horny, and when that sexual peak hit, we hit the bed of the first other man that says howdy do. *My husband didn't pay enough attention to me*—it was because he was working overtime to pay off your credit card bills, bitch, that's why. *My husband won't make love to me anymore,* it's because you got fat you dumb bitch, or because you won't eat and you're so damned skinny you remind him of Olive Oyl when you undress. *My husband is always looking at other women on TV,* it's because you're *frigid* that's why, he's got blue balls waiting for you to come around once every six weeks. *My daughter curses at me and she pushes me and she won't stop yelling at me,* maybe it's because you won't get out of her fucking face and leave her alone for five minutes. I often wonder how bad things between my computer software clown and me would have been if he had not died, and had not left me enough life insurance to take care of me and his five year old daughter for the rest of our lives. Philip Atwood, thanks a million.

My strawberry delight is in her favorite place, in the open field at twilight, as I roll into the driveway beside the house. She seems strangely focused on the eastern sky, facing toward the house instead of away as usual. When I get out of the silver SUV, I glance upward, slightly fearful of what it is I might see, but seeing nothing except the face of the Moon, Mare Luna herself, staring down at me in blatant mocking and disgust for my plight. I turn and wave at the figure far off in the distance, but to no avail. From what I can tell, she is standing still with her arms crossed, looking at the Moon rising over the field, likely imagining whatever cosmic mischief she can cause, to pass the days until the end of our time.

The carnivore inside me is grateful for this rotisserie bird I bought, my mouth nearly watering while I carry it into the house, and the new Ice Princess Barbie I picked up as a surprise, along with a Supergirl figure that caught my attention and I just had to buy. The twenty something year old blonde chippie, working part time at the toy store to pad her resume and please her mother, said to me (more like smiled and sang to me), *"oh, Ice Princess Barbie and Supergirl—how old is your little daughter?"* And in my mind I pull a .38 revolver from my purse and put it in the middle of her tiny forehead and say *"She's 27, bitch,"* and I pull the trigger and splatter her brains all over the people in the other line, and then walk out without paying for a damned thing, and get in my car and drive calmly away. But my own brain emerged quickly from this contempt, and I smile and say *"Actually she's a few years older than you... she collects them."* And then I smile and giggle my pathetic politeness in full fungalooga white, swiping my card, and waiting for my receipt as she chatters on, hardly surprised that she stares at my breasts like she is reading a sign. And remarkably, she does it above board, as if it is a right she has, as if the fact that she is a young woman herself gives her permission to look once, twice, and then a third time as I walk away. What would the little motheress wannabe have done if I had gotten her alone somewhere, opened my shirt and shoved one of them into her mouth? This, I cannot tell.

The rotisserie bird takes its place on the stove, while I go upstairs to visit the prairie doll chorus, to add number one hundred and four to their legion. In the upper room, I can feel the heavy burden of secrets too numerous to know, depravities too deep to discuss. They know of every incident, of what has darkened the corners of every room in the house, from my daughter's anal raping when she was sixteen, to the stench of my sickness in full blossom on the bathroom toilet, while she straddled me, as I released every bit of what a laxative does to the human body, groaning my gruff animal grunting while I pissed and shat, holding onto her for dear life as I passed the pain into the toilet away from me, kissing her deeply while she flushed the stench of our depravity away. If these dolls could talk, of what pain and suffering, pray tell, have they been privy and privileged to? What end of the world tragedies are they aware of? What premonitions burden their all seeing hearts and minds? What do they know of the coming eschatology?

The light of Mare Luna shines at me through my daughter's eastern window, as I place Supergirl somewhere nearby the Amazon Princess, and the girl who followed the Yellow Brick Road. I can feel my own brow wrinkle in sudden, tragic revelation, causing me to turn immediately and hurry out of the upper room.

Outside, in the twilight dark, I perceive the Alpha and the Omega. Standing in the field, having not moved a single inch since I arrived.

Staring at the Moon.

*THE TWELVE MOONS of the Northern Hemisphere*
*As they burden the heart and mind*

*January is the Mountain Moon*
*Over snowy mountain peaks*
*While February is the Glacier Moon*
*As we endure the bitter cold.*

*When days grow longer, the birds return,*
*And leaf and flower buds reappear on the trees in waiting—*
*March is the Spring Moon—*
*To bid farewell to winter*

## Venicia in the Cause of Aircraft

*And April is the River Moon*
*The month of showers*
*Watering the ground with warm weather's renewal.*
*May is the Flower Moon*
*In promises made by colors of the field—*
*To provide Earth another season of life.*

*The Twelve Moons of the Northern Hemisphere—*
*As they burden the heart and mind*

*June is the Summer Moon*
*The rule of travel and leisure,*
*Hopes of warmth and days of love—*
*And prosperity.*
*July is the Prairie Moon*
*The arrival of clear skies and open roads—*
*And the approach of new horizons ahead.*

*August is the Desert Moon*
*The rise of summertime heat*
*In the extension of hope—*
*And leisure times reborn.*
*September is the Autumn Moon*
*The return of labour's burden*
*A season of death*
*When a cool wind may whisper a warning*
*To summer's children.*

## Jonathan Lovejoy

*Rising above the planting fields*
*October is the Harvest Moon*
*Over the colors of the dying leaves*
*The time to reap the rewards of seeds sown.*
*November is the Forest Moon*
*When the leaves are taken by the autumn wind*
*As the woods gather to themselves*
*To sleep under the warm sky coalesced—*
*In rain upon their grief and mourning.*

*At the turn of these last days*
*When Death is as the icy rain*
*December is the Winter Moon*
*To hearken the final season*
*And the death and burial of nature—*

*In the cold.*

As IT IS WRITTEN, days come and go, as do the seasons. Until the earth has made another journey, and it is *summer* again.

In the year since I first had my suspicions, since I first approached her in the field, and saw the wheat swirling about, the world has come to know the meaning of fear.

The first month of this brought about worldwide delight and curiosity, as the full moon was bigger in the sky than it had been in the history of mankind. Pictures were taken ad nauseam, reports given daily for many days, with more interest in our lunar cousin than any other time in recorded history, which seemed to bring about an uneasy calm over the population, as every romantic fantasy of lunar delight was lived by many, with so much good natured talk of lunatics and lunacy, and the resurgence of werewolves in London notwithstanding. Teen wolves howled, Jack Nicholson wolves growled, Dee Wallace and other lady wolves yowled at the world through the TV screen, as people howled with delight over the foolishness of *lycanthropy*, and the giant Moon in their late summer skies. But curiously, upon the advent of Autumn, in the cloudy skies of the November Forest Moon, the world noticed that on the fifth pass of the full Moon since that July, that the Moon was *twice* the size that it had been in every human being's wildest dreams, with the world's attention drawn to astronomy's non answers, the how's and why's of how the Moon suddenly seemed to drift out of its orbit, and pass closer to the Earth every single month, with fearful speculation of what the sixth, seventh, eighth, and ninth month would bring. But as the February Glacier Moon gave way to the River Moon of April, the truth descended in revelation, as the full moon filled *one fourth* of the entire night sky, tragically visible in the daytime as well, as a faded but no less fearful representation of what tragedies threaten to come. The River Moon saw the first of the Great Earthquakes that rocked cities to their foundations, finally delivering scientific promise upon the San Andreas Fault, which did not send California into the ocean, but rather sent west coast cities into the ground in flaming ruins, as cities suffered the cataclysmic arrival of geological prophecy, sending tens of millions of souls screaming to their fiery deaths in the many cracks and fissures that opened from the fault line to the Pacific Ocean, openings hardly visible from high in the sky, but opened as gateways to the pits of Hell on the surface of the Earth. And the coastal cities were not spared the indignities of centuries of wonder and speculation fulfilled, as the waters of high tides flowed slowly inward night after night, to make the streets impassable by car or train, to render every coastal subway line useless, until they were decommissioned and abandoned before the beginning of May, when the Flower Moon brought with it the rising winds of late spring, and the formation of storm cells as have never been imagined, where the landscape was covered in small and large twisters for the better part of two weeks in tornado alley, when the skies underneath the giant Moon were covered in wind, rain and a thick veil of dark and melancholy gray. These twisters whirled and danced about from North to South, moving rapidly from West to East, some appearing over the coastal waters of the Gulf of Mexico, spinning white tranquility from the water all the way into a thousand feet of funnel cloud, to rest in the wake of its calling, as but a sign and wonder of what impossibilities must be wrought upon the earth. And over the blue lava pits of East Java, Indonesia, there appeared one angry funnel, swirling the molten blue fire up into itself at night, to cause worldwide speculation on the cause of Armageddon, and the burning of blue and black fire. From the bottom to the top of the Pacific Rim, volcanoes that modern man had never seen awakened, exploding their fiery message into the air, to fill the skies with fire and smoke, to end all hope and speculation of survival, as the fire pits rained glowing rocks from high into the skies, igniting the forests and fields along the countryside down below. Animals retreated from the highland forests, down into the brief, feeble safety of the low lying cities, killing men, women and children in fear and madness, as the ground shook day and night under the new stresses caused by the Mare Luna, and its growing proximity to the planet Earth.

They have called this the twelfth and final safe pass, as I am unable to bring myself to leave my home, to join the cause of eschatology in the new field of hopeless wheat planted, the open field of mankind's prayer for survival gone unanswered. Along with the rest of humanity, I cower in my home, paralyzed by fear, unable to bring myself to step into the hot and cold reality of Truth, that circles over *one half* of the night sky, as no longer the light that rules the night, but as the fulfillment of scripture, that the sun shall be turned to darkness, and the moon into blood, as the daytime sun is often eclipsed for half its journey across the sky, and the nighttime Moon is angry, with molten seas of lava born upon is surface, until it seems as though a Vulcan planet hurtles toward us without mercy. In this twelfth and final safe pass of the woman who rules the night, the Earth cannot cease from the shaking, the quaking of itself to ruin, as every human being has abandoned its way, ceasing the eating, drinking, the marrying and the giving in marriage, as the clouds of endtime thunder have been scattered by the howling winds, and every part of the skies are in brackish clarity, that every eye shall see her, and every tongue might confess, and every knee shall bow to Diana, Queen of the Night, as the fires and dusts of the Earth's surface have begun to spread, and sanity has begun to slowly but surely fade away.

*THE SPIRIT OF CHRIST is the spirit of love,* are the words that torment me at this moment, though the Earth rumbles like thunder, and the wind screams the chimes of a wayward jet engine plane. I get up from my sofa of fear, going to the back door, hurrying through the wind to the figure in the field of dreams, approaching the terrifying goddess with caution, feeling the power of the curtain of wind that protects her from harm.

"Venicia!"

I scream it to the top of my lungs, even as my blood runs cold from the sight of her eyes, and the pale glow that shines from them. But this creature is my daughter, which is the last rope I have upon which to grab hold, climbing up to her through the swirling wind, grabbing on to her in the rumbling of the ground, and the swirling cacophony of wind, screaming to the top of my lungs.

"Mercy! Mercy! God is love, Venicia! God is *love!*"

And with this, I feel a sudden release of the tension in her muscles, and a calming in the swirling air around us, as I see her hair begin to settle in place, as I brave a look into the whiteness of her eyes, seeing the beauty of earthen black return to the center of them, while I see humanity return to her merciless expression.

As the winds begin to quiet their dreadful voices, as the ground begins to cease its rumbling, I say to her again "God is love, Venicia. God is love."

I stand in the light of the evening day, hugging my daughter in the spirit of true love, observing the flash of a single light in the Western sky, giving a spark of hope to two souls on the open prairie, in the midst of Paradise lost, across the grieving landscape of a condemned earth down below.

## ABOUT THE AUTHOR

Jonathan Lovejoy is a graduate of the University of North Carolina at Greensboro, with a B.A. in Religious Studies, and a graduate of Liberty University with an M.A. in Theological Studies. He currently lives in Winston Salem, North Carolina.

For more info on the author's life and career, visit jonathanlovejoy.com